SPECIAL MESSAGE T

THE ULVERSCROFT F

res

You

Ev

THE ULVERSCROFT FOUNDATION
The Green, Bradgate Road, Anstey
Leicester LE7 7FU, England
Tel: (0116) 236 4325

website: www.foundation.ulverscroft.com

Sara Judge was born in Zambia, and was brought up and educated in England. She trained as a dancer and spent several years on the stage, taking part in summer shows, pantomimes and night club acts. Now retired, she enjoys spending time with her four grandchildren and attending pilates classes.

HONEY BROWN IS MARRIED

March 1950: ex-showgirl Honey Brown has married the farmer she adores — August Blake Esq. — and though she pines for the bright lights and glamour of the Windmill Theatre, her new mother-in-law, Doris, is determined to turn Honey into a respectable lady of the manor. To make matters worse, as well as the struggle to meet Doris's exacting standards, Honey feels increasing animosity towards dairyman Nick. Why does she dislike him, when everyone else seems to find him so agreeable? When enmity between the two turns to disaster, Honey wonders if her life on the farm is really worth fighting for.

SARA JUDGE

HONEY BROWN IS MARRIED

Complete and Unabridged

ULVERSCROFT
Leicester

First published in Great Britain in 2012 by
Robert Hale Limited
London

First Large Print Edition
published 2013
by arrangement with
Robert Hale Limited
London

*A catalogue record for this book is available
from the British Library.*

ISBN 978–1–4448–1751–5

Published by
F. A. Thorpe (Publishing)
Anstey, Leicestershire

Set by Words & Graphics Ltd.
Anstey, Leicestershire
Printed and bound in Great Britain by
T. J. International Ltd., Padstow, Cornwall

This book is printed on acid-free paper

For Boyana

1

March 1950 — it's a Monday
but I don't know the date!

I am so wonderfully happy! I cannot believe I am still ME and all these things are really happening.

Mrs August Blake. I write the name over and over again and every time my heart jerks and I can feel my lips smiling.

Stupid, I know, and I'll come out of this dream presently and learn to be a proper farmer's wife. My dear mother-in-law is going to teach me. I am just not good enough for her beloved son, but she will do her best to improve on such bad material, I have no doubt.

However, up till now there has not been a cloud on the horizon and after one blissful week in Wales on honeymoon, we are now home and I've taken this exercise book which I found in the cupboard under the stairs, and am going to write in it regularly and make it my diary.

I need to talk to somebody and as August is out so much during the day I shall write down all my thoughts, and all the day's happenings. I expect I shall be lonely at first, although my husband, August Blake Esq. (I can't resist that!) insists I'll soon make friends down here in Sussex. *He* knows enough people — the church was packed for our wedding and I know *my* lot only numbered about six.

I'll do my best to be friendly when I meet anyone, and give and accept invitations, but until then this book will keep me company.

Who would have thought, a bare two years ago, that I would now be sitting in this large old drawing room (*not* sitting room, please, dear. M.I.L.) with a wide gold band upon the third finger of my left hand, married to August Blake Esq?

'Don't forget the Esq, dear. You don't address any man on the envelope as plain Mr unless, of course, he is one of the tradespeople.' M.I.L.

Sorry, I didn't know that, and a lot of other things as well, but I am GOING TO LEARN.

Who would have thought that little Annie Brown, an orphan and probably illegit living in a Home for the first fifteen years of her life, then performing on stage with the stunning name of Honey Brown (my idea), would end up leading such a respectable existence?

Who would have thought I would have

been capable of attracting such a man as August? And that he would have fallen in love with me and vice versa — but oh, so vice versa! And that I would have achieved the unbelievable and become his wife!

Still can't believe it — neither can my mother-in-law, but she puts on a brave face at present. Hope it lasts. I'm quite prepared to be agreeable. I don't say I'll love her as my own, but I will *like* her with determination if she will leave me alone and not interfere too much.

Luckily she lives down in the village and the farm is some three miles from there. But Mil is a devil on her bicycle and I rather dread hearing the bang of the kitchen door and her voice raised in greeting.

I know I'm pretty dumb and I've a lot of learning to do, and I'll accept criticism and knowledge gracefully so long as it's not doled out in large amounts. And so long as she is kind. A cruel tongue is very hard to forgive.

Matron was kind and meant well, I can see that now, but she had such a biting tongue, such a sharp and sarcastic way of saying things, we were all scared of her and longed to be 'grown up' and allowed to leave the Home.

* * *

3

I was lucky with my dancing. And with Auntie. They got me out of that bleak red building and, apart from being a healthy and interesting pastime, dancing gave me the training for a career later in life.

I went to Miss Griggs' School of Dance all through the war years. Her first studio was only ten minutes' walk from the Home and I went on Tuesday and Thursday afternoons and had to hurry back before the blackout, with my gas mask banging against my thigh in its canvas box. *Such* annoying things — we never had to use them but always had to carry them with us.

The bigger girls used to stay on later for their classes but Matron expected me back before the lights went out, and I never dared to disobey her although I longed to stay on after my class and watch the more difficult exercises at the barre and the enchainement of the elementary students.

It was also VERY annoying when a bomb fell right next door to Miss Griggs' studio. Luckily it was at night, she didn't sleep there and the folk next door were down in their Anderson shelter in the garden so no one was hurt.

But there followed weeks of boredom and frustration for me as Miss Griggs searched for new accommodation and I tried to practise in the bedroom, with little space. There was also no music, no one to watch me and nobody giving me orders. Eventually, to my joy, Matron told me that another place had been found, still in Earls Court but further away from the Home.

I remember Auntie coming to collect me. I think everyone was glad when I went back to my classes, and after showing me the way to and from the Home, I was then allowed to go on my own as before.

How I loved those hours spent at Miss Griggs', and how I hated having to return to that cold building for high tea of bread and marge and warm milk.

It was awful leaving the brightly lit studio, with the tinkling magic of the piano, the human smell of the dressing room and the laughter and chatter of the other girls.

She helped me a lot, Miss Griggs, in those early years and so did Auntie. Kind old ladies, both of them, and both at my wedding on Saturday, 11th March — I won't ever forget that date! They made me feel I did have *some* family. And Lyn came, and Mrs Goddard, and Henry. But Matron didn't come. I suppose she was too busy but I'm glad I sent her an invitation. I got a jolly nice vase from her (probably from Woollies) and brought down by Miss Griggs. It has fresh clean colours — blue and white and splashes of yellow. There's a big bunch of daffodils sitting in it today, found beside the track leading up to our house, and so golden and bright I couldn't resist picking them.

Funny, really, after being a dancer at the Windmill Theatre and happily taking off my clothes and wearing loads of make-up and ostrich plumes and high heels, I now sink into the cosy warmth (in the kitchen) of farmhouse tranquillity with no audience to impress, just a tall quiet man whom I adore.

And I am stirred by the bold splash of gold in the grass. Oh yes, and the cats! More of them later.

God must laugh sometimes at the strange complexities in our characters; to see how often we try to be what we are not whilst He sees everyone and everything in its true colours and shapes.

* * *

I'm rambling now — I always know when I should stop talking, or writing — that's when I get onto religion. I'm a religious person in a way, I suppose. I believe in God and say my prayers most nights (when I'm not too tired) as we were taught to do in the Home. And I believe most firmly in Heaven and a lovely get-together at the last.

I must believe this because I have to see my parents. I have to know what they were like and whether I take after my mother, or my father. And did they have any other children? Have I got brothers and sisters somewhere out there in the world? I wish I knew. But as I do not, I just have to believe in the Hereafter when all will be made clear to me.

I am not particularly churchy, though. That all depends on the vicar. But I haven't met an attractive one yet. And if a man doesn't attract me I don't see why I should go to his church and sit for an hour on my bottom listening to dull words spewing out from a dreary personality. That has nothing to do with God, I'm sure.

I really will stop now. They used to call me Mrs Billy Graham in the theatre, because I was always getting involved in religious tirades about Jews and animals. Cruelty to defenceless creatures really makes me wild.

One Sunday in Leeds when we were rehearsing for the Christmas panto of *Mother Goose*, three of us girls were playing cards in the dressing room during a break. Then there was a knock on the door and in marches an R.C. priest. Did everybody's face get red!

But I don't know why, because we weren't sinning even if it was a Sunday. Anyway, I invited the Father to join us. He was nice, good looking and young and didn't seem upset by my dressing gown hanging open and showing my bra and fishnets. But he said he wouldn't butt in, just wanted to know if there were any R.Cs present. There weren't.

This annoyed me. After all, they are against the colour bar and that kind of prejudice but if you aren't of their faith, you are nothing. I asked him a lot of questions in a rather belligerent tone — I nearly said I was an orphaned bastard and how did he feel about that? But I didn't.

It can't have been easy for him with Bella and Josie sitting there grinning, and me smoking and coughing, and the air all heavy and fuggy. And all kinds of clothing and underwear scattered around the hot room.

Make-up, powder, removal cream, cotton wool, all mixed up with cigarettes and ash trays and pieces of wet soap. Rather different to a presbytery, I should think. We offered him a chair but he remained standing, a slight, pale figure in black, with a face like a Renaissance knight. Then he went away.

I know all about the Renaissance — something else people aren't going to believe. Because August is very interested in that sort of thing, and when we were in Wales he had a book with him with lovely pictures and engravings. He used to read me bits at night when we were snuggled up in bed.

It sounds silly but I enjoyed it. He has a nice voice for listening to — quiet and deep, and he explained as he went along so I was with him most of the time and not falling asleep from boredom.

Fancy taking a book on honeymoon! I can just imagine what cracks the girls would have made about that. But they will never know and that week was bliss. Just him and me and bits of the Renaissance.

I'm stopping now, I really am.

2

Wednesday evening

My mother-in-law popped in this afternoon. She had cycled up from the village. That's something I must learn soon — how to ride a bicycle.

I asked if she would like a cup of tea but she said she'd just had one. She had a little poke around but I didn't mind much. I've changed nothing so everything is more or less as she left it.

I asked her what I should call her and she said 'Mother' in that brisk way of hers. But I can't do that. She isn't a bit like I imagine a mother to be. I'm quite sure mine wasn't like her. So I speak in careful sentences and have avoided the issue so far.

I could call her Mil, but I don't suppose she'd like that. Or Doris. That's her name but everyone calls her Mrs Blake — except August, of course. He says Mother, but it sounds awfully stiff to me. If a mother is really warm and gentle and loving she'd have to be Mum, or Mam, or Mummy. Mother isn't right at all. But it does suit Mil so perhaps I will call her that after a while.

I'll practise first and then it might slip out without me even thinking about it.

Mil wanted to know what Mrs Stow is doing each day. Am I keeping an eye on her? Giving her enough to do?

The answer is No, but I didn't say that.

We marched into the kitchen together, Mrs Stow goes off at 12 o'clock and doesn't come in again until 8 o'clock next morning. Then Mil inspected the stove and sink, saw that there was enough wood and coal in the box for the range and trailed her inquisitive finger over the dresser and table top. No dust. Mrs Stow was in luck.

I like her and often go in and have a chat and a coffee at around 11. I bring my tin of Nescafé with me; Mrs Stow had never seen instant before. There's none down here so I'll have to think of a way to get some more.

When she makes coffee there's all that palaver of coffee beans and having to grind them, and pour boiling water over them in a jug, and all that *waiting*. And it's always too weak and watery because of the rationing and coffee beans are scarce, etc. etc. I do like my coffee strong and instant, and lovely Nescafé is all that. But how do I get hold of some more?

I hate tea. Well, I don't mind it at *tea time*

but that's all, thank you very much.

Anyway, I can't imagine inspecting Mrs Stow's work and telling her this is wrong, or that could be done better. How could I? She doesn't even call me Mrs Blake — it's either Mrs August, or sometimes it's duck.

She and I have a good natter at the kitchen table and a smoke. She has her Woodbines and I've brought my Peter Stuyvesant with me, but am going to run out soon and must see if *they* are available at the village store. Mrs Stow seems to think they are but very expensive, she says.

She makes delicious scones and pastries, I must watch my weight, and always leaves us some home-made goodies in the larder for our supper, as well as cooking our lunch before she goes.

Yippee! I'm not exactly a dab hand at cooking although I do roast for August on Sundays. The roast midday is easy and I don't believe it *can* go wrong. Mrs Stow has told me exactly what to do and so far I haven't made a mistake and August is pleased.

I'm dying for some mushrooms. August says I must go out into the fields in autumn and pick them early in the morning. Home-grown mushrooms — now *that's* a thought! But not for breakfast. I'm not a breakfast person — Mrs Stow does that for

August when she comes in at 8. But I'll cook them for supper and we'll have them with bacon. Yum.

Mrs Stow is a clever cook and makes everything go a long way. Of course, living on a farm we are lucky with eggs and butter and milk. But sugar is a problem and Mrs Stow is very cautious with that. Thank goodness I don't take it in either coffee or tea.

* * *

When Mil asked where my Menu Book was, I looked at her blankly and said I didn't know.

'You don't know, child? What in the world have you been eating these last days? I had it all written up for you and left it in the pigeonhole in your writing desk. Haven't you looked?'

I didn't know I had a writing-desk and certainly hadn't peered into any pigeonholes.

We marched back into the *drawing room* with Mil leading and me following. There Mil advanced on a nice little antique desk which had a key sticking out of the top sloping area. I had never dared to open it, but apparently this is now mine and I was shown writing paper, and envelopes, all nicely headed with the address of the farm.

I must write to Matron — it'll kill her!

And there was a row of pigeonholes with places for bills and receipts, address book, telephone book, an account book (???) and, of course, a scarlet bound volume marked Menu Book, in Mil's neat writing, with various headings for Visitors, Overnight Guests and Weekly, plus normal daily variations.

She showed me a batch of stiff white cards.

'I write these up every Sunday evening and give one to Mrs Stow on Monday morning. Then she knows how to cope and budget for the entire week. Pay close attention to your accounts, dear. With so much produce from the farm there is little that needs to be bought. Phone your order through on Monday morning and Mr Williams' van delivers each Tuesday. The store's telephone number is here, dear.'

I thanked her, casting a nervous glance at her capable square-tipped hands, which were shuffling and setting to rights the paper in those gaping pigeonholes.

No more ready-for-the-oven pies left by Mrs Stow, I said to myself. You'd better spend the morning sitting at your desk and playing at being mistress of the mansion.

It all seemed so unnecessary. August and I had been plodding along quite happily with Mrs Stow's cooking up till now, leaving her to do whatever she wished. But I didn't want to antagonize Mil so nodded gratefully and said I would arrange the menus for the following week according to the instructions in her smoothly scarlet book.

'Engagements are written in here.' A dark blue leather volume was thrust at me. 'I don't suppose you will have any just yet but you would do well to keep track of anything August has on. He is hopelessly vague at times, and needs a practical wife to see he doesn't forget anything. Jot down any meetings, market days, vet's visits, etc. and I'm sure he'll be delighted when you remind him of something he might otherwise have forgotten.'

She asked if I wound up the grandfather clock in the hall and seemed satisfied when I said No, I left that to August.

Yes, Mil, no, Mil, three bags full, Mil. You old bag.

I mustn't be nasty and really am grateful that she is taking an interest in me but I don't want her to visit *too* often.

What I like best is lying on my bed with a good book, a packet of cigarettes and the company of a cat, or two, if they can make it up the stairs without Mrs Stow seeing them.

But what would Mil think, and *say*, if she caught me!

I suppose it would be more sensible to stay

in the front bedroom and then I'd hear her voice in the kitchen below. But the back room has always been August's — it *smells* like him (when I get rid of the cigarette smoke) and it's rough and a bit untidy and cosy. We've moved in another bed and are fine there. I've put most of my clothes in the wardrobe next door and we manage beautifully.

But I know we should really be in the front room. It's large and spacious and rather nicely decorated with striped wallpaper. There's a little spindly chair with elegant legs (no good for August!) with a striped seat like the wallpaper. There's even a big double bed and I suppose it would be much more proper if we retired there at night.

But it is a very feminine room and was Mil's before August and I got married, and I don't like the idea of putting my body down where *she* has lain. There's a thick sheepskin rug beside the bed *and* a pink hand basin. I think I'll keep it for visitors and go on as we are at the back — a little cramped but comfy.

I don't suppose Mil knows as yet. She hasn't been upstairs and I can't believe she'll ask where we sleep.

Whilst I'm at it I'll describe the house. It's fairly old — a bit beamy in the hall — but don't know when it was built, haven't learnt that yet. And there's no interesting date engraved over the front door — like 1066 or 1610.

On the outside it's half-wood and brick-work. The wood is painted white and the boards go up to the roof. The bottom half is all red brick.

It's odd inside, rambling and impractical with lots of stone floors downstairs, all humpy and bumpy. Except the kitchen which is smoothly tiled. Upstairs, the wooden floors are rough and uneven and creak. Hence, old.

There's the one big front bedroom then a long passage leading to a small lav at the end, and beside it on the left a box room or store room. The other end of the passage leads to the landing then bends back sharply to the second passage which passes the two back bedrooms and ends with a FREEZING bathroom plus lav for our part of the house.

At Mil's end you have to wash in the pink hand basin, or else come trooping along this draughty corridor, turn and follow the other passage from the landing down to the icy bathroom.

Visitors can have Mil's old room (pink) and when we have a baby it can have the bedroom next to ours. I shall call it July.

August says No, but I am quite determined. That name would suit either a boy or girl, and I think ours will be a most whimsical family. August and Honey beget (as they say in the Bible) July. It sounds all right with Blake, too. July Blake. That's all right.

I can't think how po-faced Doris Blake chose such a quaint name for her son (although I do like it), but apparently it's a family name on *her* side dating back to her grandfather.

Poor old August's dad didn't have a say at all. He was a gentle, quiet man — so I've heard — a bit like August (although August can be quite fierce sometimes) and it didn't matter what Mr Blake's grandfather had been called, Doris's son was going to be christened August and that was that.

Wonder what she will have to say about July?

3

Friday

The vicar's wife called this morning. I had on my bright red top and satiny slacks — Henry always admired them and I felt like cheering myself up. I'd just washed my hair, too, so it was all bubbly and fluffy and looking especially nice although it was wasted on her.

Pity the vicar didn't come.

Mrs Dawson looked a bit askance and sat rigidly on one of the armchairs rather forward and unrelaxed, trying not to stare at my scarlet top, which does show off a bit of cleavage.

She perched uncomfortably in her heavy tweed suit and great rubber-soled shoes. We didn't have a great deal in common. She has never been to London and I know she was wondering if I was a dyed blonde.

Actually I am (must remember to check on my bottle of peroxide). Is there a hairdresser in the village? And how do I get there and back? Nobody guessed that I was dyed — not even August — but then he hasn't a clue about such things.

I glided through to the kitchen and asked Mrs Stow for tea and biscuits. She had just made a batch of her fabulous scones so I asked for a few of those as well, with butter and jam. She said we were short on jam, have to wait till the summer and she'll make some more, but there was plenty of butter and with the scones still warm from the oven, the butter went well with them. Yum.

Mrs Dawson didn't do more than crumble one biscuit between her long, nervy fingers but I finished the scones. Country air is terrible for my appetite and I'm cutting back on ciggies because I don't know when I can get some more. Anyway, the vicar's wife drank two cups of tea so she must have felt a bit at ease, or else thirsty after her ride up from the village.

We sat in the drawing room. Normally I slum it in the hall, or kitchen, if I'm not reading on my bed. The hall's an odd room with the stairs leading out of it, so it's invariably draughty but there's an enormous open fire in it, and lots of unpresentable furniture like a sagging sofa and huge (ditto) armchair. The big noisy grandfather clock is in one corner, and it's where August allows the dogs. He always says the cats must remain OUT. Most unfair, as I far prefer cats and try to allow one or two in and pretend I haven't seen them.

The hall sofa and chair are comfortable and shabby. It's an untidy sort of room which leads to the kitchen, but you can sit and put your feet up there and, once winter comes round, I shall read there as I'm sure the bedroom will be too cold.

Back to Mrs Dawson. She rang the front door bell and I opened it with difficulty. The wood must have warped and we use it very seldom. It was quite a battle to wrench it open and smile at the lady visitor.

She was my first apart from Mil. But Mil doesn't count as she always comes in through the kitchen. Then we sat ourselves down on either side of the empty fireplace and I pulled out the electric heater and switched on one bar. It was rather damp and cold in there.

It was a relief when Mrs Stow bustled in with the tray of tea things and set them on the little table beside me. I poured out and offered plates and tried to look like a good hostess.

Unfortunately, Ming, one of the cats, slipped in with Mrs Stow and came and wound herself around Mrs Dawson's lisle stockings. She didn't care for cats, she told me, flinching, and there had been none in the house when August's mother lived there.

I rose and went to pick Ming up.

'I can't resist them,' I said brightly, sitting down again with Ming curling gratefully on my lap. 'I take several to bed with me each night and August doesn't mind at all. We have seven on the farm and I have given them all names, little darlings.'

Ming stiffened slightly as I crooned, she wasn't used to such extreme devotion.

'I'm afraid I don't like dogs much,' I went on, as Mrs Dawson remained silent. 'Especially when they get old and fat and smelly. Cocker spaniels are the worst offenders but terriers aren't much better.'

I knew that much about dogs because Miss Laycock used to bring Queenie, her old spaniel, to the Home with her every day and it used to sleep in a fat snuffling lump beside her chair. When it died, she brought along Bertie, a terrier which had been rescued from a bomb site.

Mrs Dawson didn't stay long after that. As she collected her bicycle from beside the kitchen wall, she informed me with a false smile that she would be holding a little tea party at the vicarage next Tuesday afternoon at four. If I should care to come, she would introduce me to the neighbourhood.

I said I didn't have transport but if I could persuade August to give me a lift in his truck,

I would come. She said maybe Lydia Dickinson, the district nurse, could pass my way in her car. It would depend on her round that day, but she would let me know. I said thank you, so we'll wait and see.

I'll try it once. Wish I could cycle, then I would be independent. Must talk to August about getting a bike.

* * *

Almost forgot — I found a hedgehog this morning before I washed my hair. The dogs were making a terrific racket so I went out to see what was the matter and there he was — rolled up in a tight little ball on the front lawn, with both dogs worrying him and barking ferociously.

I grabbed them by their collars and dragged them away. Luckily they know me and didn't snap although Wolf always looks vicious with her yellow eyes. I shut her and Reg in the side shed and went to investigate.

The hedgehog — a tiny prickly bundle — wasn't hurt. I wrapped an old piece of sacking around him and carried him in to show Mrs Stow.

I had never seen one before and was delighted when he unrolled himself on the kitchen floor and began snuffling around exploring on his funny little legs.

Mrs Stow laughed and said I'd better watch out for fleas. I put down a saucer of milk and after a while he drank it. I was so pleased. They are fascinating little creatures with soft underbellies and little black hands. He had an adorable black nose and I would have kept him if it hadn't been for those wretched dogs. Hunters, both of them. Give me a cat any day. Though (whisper, whisper) mice and birds would say cats were hunters, too.

I took a bucket from the scullery and rolled the hedgehog into it then set off for the nearest wood, leaving the dogs still imprisoned and barking furiously behind me.

I found a nice dry ditch on the outskirts of the wood and tipped him into it. I do hope he'll be safe there. I wonder what natural enemies hedgehogs have? I must ask August. But not today.

When I got back he was standing by the gate and so CROSS because I'd shut the dogs in and they'd been making such a row. After he'd stalked away with the dogs following him, I scuttled into the house and washed my hair and put on my snazzy red top and satin slacks. Both good for my morale.

That was when Mrs Dawson came calling.

It's not all that easy being a farmer's wife.

4

Wednesday morning

I've been. Yesterday afternoon at four o'clock. August dropped me off at the vicarage and that Lydia Dickinson phoned earlier to say she would give me a lift back afterwards, as it was on her way to someone-or-other.

It wasn't as bad as I had feared and I'm glad I went — met some interesting people, all female, and two smelly spaniels.

The vicar popped his head round the door and asked if we were enjoying ourselves and, like dutiful children, we all chorused 'Yes'! then giggled self-consciously. He's much nicer than his wife. Not much for looks — not a Renaissance knight — but a kind, round face with warm eyes. He's a twinkling bustling little man, whereas she is thin and tall and angular and always wears the same nondescript tweed suit and heavy shoes.

The vicar chatted to me for a bit — I remembered him from my wedding — and he asked after August and muttered, 'Very good, very good,' several times.

I believe one could call him a real Christian

— not prejudiced in any way — unlike her. I think I could have worn my red blouse or a swimsuit, or even a see-through blouse, and he would have acted in the same way muttering 'Very good, very good,' and would have been genuinely interested in me as a *person*, not caring at all how I looked.

His wife is quite different. It is all appearance and family with her, and as I have too much of the one and none at all of the other, I'm not very popular. She was polite, all right, and introduced me round, but forgot all about me after that and spent most of the time chatting to Mil. They call each other Doris and Phyllis but everyone else says Mrs to them.

I had been very careful to dress the part of Mrs August Blake, so Old Ma Dobson should have been satisfied. I wore a particularly ugly bulky old skirt which I had been meaning to throw out for ages. With it, I wore a twinset in pale pink (which Mil gave me. I hate pink!) and two rows of pearls which I bought with one of my first pay packets from Woollies. They still look good and I felt like Lady Muck.

In the front room of the vicarage — drawing room? Sitting room? Parlour? — it was very depressing with lots of beige and brown and heavy furniture, and dreary prints on the walls of stags and sailing ships. There were nine of us females, plus the two ancient spaniels — don't know their sex.

Two of the women are still very vague, I can't remember their names, but the others were Mrs Silver, the chemist's wife, about as old as Mil and Mrs Dawson. They both dressed in the same tweedy way. Then there was Lydia Dickinson, district nurse, who was in a dark blue uniform with crisp white collar and cuffs, and black hair scraped back into a bun and sturdy black shoes. No make-up, of course, and she had removed her navy hat.

Lydia Dickinson had a brusque manner and a clipped way of speaking, but her eyes were kind. Large and brown, like a cow, I think I could like her if I ever got to know her well. And if she'd let me. The barrier is up at present. I am a showgirl, for heaven's sake. But perhaps we can talk in the car?

One girl *did* dislike me. I could feel it wafting across the room in waves — no, breakers of dislike! I wonder why? Must look into the matter.

Her name is Jean Somebody-or-Other, didn't catch it. She's not married — no ring — and is a school mistress at a private school outside the village, and about my age.

Attractive and nicely dressed in a good

quiet way. Soft blue woollen dress and very good legs in lisle stockings, and smart shoes. Hmm. She has velvety brown hair drawn back into a heavy bun at the nape of her neck. Awfully school-marmish and old fashioned but it suits her. Not like Nurse Dickinson's tight little bun.

She has a lovely skin but evil eyes. Like a snake's, they are flat and grey.

Maybe I'm jealous. This Jean is a natural beauty — no make-up or peroxide for her. Nothing dazzling and artificial like Honey neé Brown. Just quietly beautiful and knows it. Very self-assured. Everything I am not.

I suppose I know I'm attractive but there's always a little bit of uncertainty somewhere down in my tum, because everything I have and am is fake. I don't mean *inside* — I'm not a liar or cheat and I really, really love August. I'm also very fond of Auntie and Lyn and Henry.

But my *outside* is false.

My hair is naturally mousey; my mouth is too big and my eyes are too small, so I am constantly fiddling and fixing and making use of all the bottles and jars I possess.

The end result is good. I don't believe my worst enemy would call me plain. But it's all worked for and carefully designed unlike that Jean person, who sat there all smooth and superior and effortlessly feminine and perfect.

Apparently she has Tuesday afternoons free so could spare the time to come. I don't know anything about term-times, or school holidays — did we have them at the Home? But when we have little July I'll have to learn all about the necessary dates — hope it won't be the school where Miss Snake-Eyes teaches, though.

Getting back to looks — the only time I really didn't care at all was on honeymoon. We were right by the sea in a funny little hotel full of elderly folk — their first holiday since the war, perhaps? And nobody knew me down there in Wales.

It was gloriously sunny but with a *bitter* wind, and the sun and sea air did wonders for my hair and skin. I didn't need any make-up and August was completely happy with me, so I could relax and just be my natural self for those seven days.

I wonder if Jean is an old flame of August's? That might explain her antagonism. She was chatting a lot to Mil and Mrs Dawson, as if she knew them well. She was born and brought up in the village, apparently, so she's been around for a long time right under August's nose.

He must have noticed her snakey eyes and

lovely complexion. No male could be unaware of her. But August Blake (Esq.) asked *me* to marry him. So yah, boo, sucks, Miss Blue Wool, Smart Shoes, Snakey-Eyes, Perfection!

* * *

The one person I did like very much was the vet's wife, Betty Folder. She's young and enthusiastic and dresses extremely badly. She came over right away and sat next to me and seemed genuinely glad to meet me. I almost thought she was going to hug me.

'I'm so glad you've come,' she said, wrapping her numerous folds of skirt around her plump legs and then sitting on her hands like an excited child. 'We need new blood in the village. Most of the young girls get jobs in Horsham, or go to Brighton, or some other town. We are left with rather a lot of elderly people,' (she lowered her voice) 'although there are some young marrieds but they are ever so taken up with having babies.

'I've been longing for some company. And dancing on the stage in London? Wow! You must tell me all about your life and I'll try not to be envious. Jean's all right, but she works late in the evening preparing and correcting homework, and my husband is often called out. They are both busy during the day, anyway, and I get lonely. Mum lives in Horsham and is spending a few days with us so is babysitting this afternoon.'

When Betty paused for breath, I managed to say, 'Is your baby a boy or girl?'

'A boy, Jerry, and he's ten months. Have you a bike, by the way? And do you ride? Horses, I mean.'

I shook my head. 'No, to both. But I'm hoping to get a bicycle soon — I must remind August. I'm not sure about horses, though.'

I am a cat person, and heaving myself up onto some enormous moving beast doesn't appeal at all.

But Betty was not daunted by my remark. 'I'll get you on a horse, Honey,' she said with a grin, 'but best to concentrate on a bike at first. You can't sit around in that old house with your sewing and knitting, and you're not a gardener, are you?'

I shook my head again. Gardening is like cooking. I like the end result and would quite like to do it but have no idea how to. Anyway, I've got Mrs Stow to do things for me.

'Thought not,' said Betty cheerfully. 'So start with cycling and then you can get out and about on your own. Be nice for me, too. I'm awfully stuck now that Jerry's come and the bus times don't fit into his feeding schedule at all.'

We arranged that she would come up and see me the following week. Another visitor — but somebody young this time. I'm looking forward to that.

'I'll come on Randy,' said Betty. 'He's my Exmoor pony. I'll bed Jerry down in your house and then we can have a good old chin-wag.'

'I'd like that,' I said, 'but how can you bring your son on horseback?'

'Papoose — style. The village nearly had a fit when they first saw me but they're used to the sight now and think it a brilliant idea. My son is going to be an expert horseman, Honey. He was practically born in the saddle, and has been with me on Randy since he was eight weeks old.'

I do like her. I've met a few oddities in the theatre but I don't think I've ever met such a refreshingly different person as Betty Folder. We are going to be friends, I know. Just what I need down here.

Betty's small and plump with very rosy cheeks and naturally fair hair, which is rather wild. Her lipstick was badly put on and clashed with her cheeks. I think she must be a very careless person but she's so warm and friendly I can't help liking her.

She told me she had jumped at the chance to get out of the house *on her own*. Thank God for mums, she said.

That made me feel sad, although I didn't show it. I wish I knew what my mother had been like. Would she have been proud of me? Would she have liked August? Would she have taught me how to be a good wife and mother?

Don't know. Never mind. I'll make sure I am a really good one when little July comes along. I'll listen to what Betty says whenever I see her, and learn from her what a good mother should do. Then everyone will say, 'You know that new Mrs August Blake? She is a remarkable lady. Although she was only a dancer at the Windmill Theatre, she has turned into a most accomplished wife and mother.'

5

Saturday

Henry came for the day yesterday! I couldn't believe my *ears* when I heard his voice on the phone saying, 'I'm sitting here at Horsham station. Shall I look for a taxi, or will you come and get me?'

I told him August was away at a sale in Lewes. Just as well. He doesn't care for Henry even though he only met him that once at our wedding. I told Henry there was a bus from the station which would drop him off at our village, but it was rather a long walk up from the bus stop. Henry doesn't like walking so he said he'd try for a taxi.

He had been to our village once before, for the wedding but had never been to the farm. Then, he'd come down with Lyn and her mother, and Auntie and Miss Griggs, and they'd all shared a taxi from Horsham.

What a hectic day that wedding had been, with Henry in a rush to get back to London, and me surrounded by so many people — all friends of the Blakes but strangers to me.

Then the hurried reception in the church

hall with Mil bossing everyone about, and me longing to get away with August, and having to change in the lav at the back of the hall, and Mil taking my bridal gown and sorting out taxis for everyone, and them all waiting for us to leave first. Phew.

I wouldn't like to go through all that again. Then the getting away with *three* different trains. One to Victoria, then one to Swansea, which we almost missed, and then spending the night at the Station Hotel (very uncomfortable and noisy) and the final little puffing billy which carried us along the coast to our honeymoon hotel.

It was on the Gower Peninsula, August said, and the beaches were golden and beautiful. I hadn't seen such glorious sandy beaches before.

I remember before the war going in a small group down to Brighton. But the cobbles hurt my feet and there was a cold wind blowing off a grey sea, and I hated it.

This day trip was supposed to be a treat for the girls who had behaved really well during the long winter months, so I made sure I was not chosen again.

Dancing, I loved. Cold, wet days by the seaside, I did not.

Next spring, when those special days were being planned in the Home, I managed to do things which were considered 'naughty' by Matron.

They weren't very bad but I pinched Susan Wood when we were getting up from lunch one day, and made her cry. She was one of Matron's favourites, so that was fine. And, just to make sure, I called fat, pudding-faced Hannah, a Hippopotamus, so she slapped my face and I slapped her back.

Because *I* had started the rumpus, my name was not put forward for another special treat, much to my joy. But then the war came and all such frivolous expeditions were stopped, anyway.

But this March, as August's bride, with the golden beaches and peace and quiet of the Gower Peninsula surrounding us, it was pure Heaven.

* * *

Back to Henry.

He said I should stand outside the house waving a white hankie so he'd feel welcomed. I did, too, much to the dogs' and the taxi driver's delight.

Then I shut the dogs out (good thing August wasn't there) and took in Henry plus three cats. He, like me, abhors dogs, but is rather partial to anything feline. Mrs Stow was thrilled. This was the first visitor I'd had to lunch and I think she wanted to show off to the gentleman from London.

She bustled away into the kitchen, all pink cheeks and enthusiasm, and donned a bright cherry-coloured apron which I hadn't seen before.

I showed off, too, and produced Mil's scarlet leather Menu Book to find out what visitors should eat on a Friday. It was plaice with green peas and boiled potatoes, followed by lemon soufflé and cream.

We didn't have any fish — I hadn't ordered any — and there were no lemons, either. Sorry, Mil. So we ended up having a nice roast leg of lamb (really for Sunday but August needn't know — I'll do slices in gravy) with roast pots and onions and yummy mint sauce — one of Mrs Stow's specialities — and lashings of gravy. She also made a very acceptable sponge pudding which we had with cream.

It was lovely seeing Henry again (August doesn't even like me *talking* about him) and we have so many shared memories about my dancing, it was a joy to chat. He arrived just after eleven so whilst Mrs Stow was busy in the kitchen I showed him round the house.

He was most taken with the front bedroom. He liked the pink hand basin and striped wallpaper and chair. I told him he could sleep there if he ever came for an overnight stay but he wasn't too keen on that idea.

'I'm sure your husband is a dear chap and an excellent farmer, darling, but we really have nothing in common and I don't fancy spending more than a few hours with you in your cosy little homestead.'

I did understand. Then we went downstairs and I showed him the drawing room and my nice writing desk and he was suitably impressed. Then we returned to the hall and he admired the grandfather clock. We put our feet up; Henry had a whisky and I had a ciggy.

He nattered away, telling me all the news about everybody — there are very few people in the business who Henry doesn't know. Well, an agent should know everything if he's to get on and I could hardly believe I had been away for over a month already.

'*The King's Rhapsody* is packing them in at the Palace,' said Henry. 'People are so sick of all the post-war austerity they adore Ivor's colour and pageantry.'

'Don't say too much or I'll get homesick,' I said, giving Ming a comforting stroke as she reclined on my knee.

Henry ignored me.

'You would make a splendid understudy for Vanessa Lee,' he said. 'You'd have to have singing lessons, of course, but that girl stops the show every night with 'Some Day my Heart will Awake'. I often think of you, Honey, when I see her.'

'Tell me about Lyn,' I said quickly, lighting up another fag. At least my friend was far away in Paris and too distant for me to envy.

Henry told me she was doing very well with the Bluebell Girls. Lyn had always wanted to join them and, once I had left the Windmill, she grabbed the opportunity to leave, too, and Henry got her in easily enough. Lyn's a real looker and has fabulous legs which are so essential in the troupe. She is also tall, so that helps.

I did wonder a little about Mrs Goddard. Lyn had always lived with her mother in London, even when she was at the Windmill, so I hoped Mrs Goddard wasn't missing her too much.

It was great to hear that she was settling down happily in France, though, and Henry gave me her address so I must write to her. On my headed notepaper. She'll choke over that!

Henry looked so odd sitting there opposite me in the sagging armchair, I had to laugh, and it took my mind off Mrs Goddard and the stage.

'What's up?' he said, all black eyes and quivery nose in his thin pale face.

'You,' I said. 'You are so nattily dressed in your navy blazer and light trousers — all wrong for the farm — and sitting in that shabby old chair with cats leaving their hair all over you.'

He grinned.

'I had to see how you were getting on, Honey, and I had a blazing row with Jessie Lane yesterday which left me feeling thoroughly stale and bad-tempered. What you need is a whiff of country air, my lad, I told myself. Go down and see how that silly child is managing amongst the cows and cabbages.

'So I left all business deals hanging and told Leila not to expect me in the office today, and slept better than I've done for months. Then I hopped on a train at Victoria this morning and here I am. Sorry you don't care for my apparel.'

Henry looked down at his cat-haired navy jacket and beautifully pressed beige trousers. His shirt was lime green, so were his socks, and his tie was yellow.

'I thought these were good country colours. But perhaps I would have done better in my purple trousers?'

How different he was to August, and how out of place.

Henry is neat and small and colourful, whereas August is all long and brown and corduroy and gumboots.

I smiled again and offered Henry another whisky. Mrs Stow rang the sheep bell promptly at one o'clock — she had stayed on an extra hour, bless her — and we sat at the kitchen table with her clucking over us.

We do have a dining room behind the hall, with a rather splendid long table and oak chairs. But it is very formal and dark in there and I have never had a meal, or even stood for long, in that cold, hostile chamber. The only time I go in is to grab a book from one of the shelves and leap out again.

Henry didn't mind slumming it. He came back for seconds twice and Mrs Stow beamed. Then I told her she must go home, and Henry insisted on drying up whilst I washed. I never knew he was so domesticated. I told him he should get married, that he'd make a marvellous husband — but he just *looked* at me for answer.

I think he's queer. But I've never been too sure about that and Lyn thinks so, too. He obviously likes female company and I've been to one or two terrific parties at his flat. But he lives alone and has never had a companion so long as I have known him.

After we'd finished clearing up in the kitchen, I showed him our larder where there is a splendid marble shelf which keeps things cool. We don't have a meat-safe — but as the larder faces north and the little window (meshed) is kept open all the time — meat and milk and butter etc. remain perfectly fresh until eaten.

Then we went outside and I showed Henry round the farm.

Unfortunately, boots were the problem. Henry has small feet but even if I had had a spare pair they wouldn't have been right for him, and August's spares were *far* too big, even with thick socks added.

'Don't worry,' said Henry, after an exhaustive search — 'I'll hop.'

And hop, he did, from patch to patch. Luckily there had been no rain for some days so there were plenty of dry patches, except for outside the milking parlour, which is sluiced down after every milking.

I don't know who was the most apprehensive — Henry or the cows. They were queuing up to go into the milking parlour and had never seen a vision in lime green and navy before. Henry kept muttering that he wasn't too keen on cattle, but he stayed with me, hopping, as I displayed my scant knowledge of the yard.

We have Jerseys. I found that out some time ago. Good for creamy milk, apparently, and they are pretty little creatures, pale beige with dark faces and feet. A bit like Siamese cats, I suppose — but no blue eyes — and with white rings around their noses.

Dairyman Nick was calling them in for milking, and there was the hum of machinery coming through the open door behind him. But as I don't like him much I just nodded and led Henry on to the barn to see the calves.

Dear little things, they are so friendly and love to suck your fingers and lick with their rough tongues. Only females — heifers, they're called — as all the boys have to go away to market. I try not to think about them being eaten, so I called the cats and introduced them to Henry.

Thank goodness it was nice and dry in the barn. He had met the tamer cats in the house, but the others are responding well to my coaxing and stroking, and Henry far preferred them to our pedigree herd.

After that I wanted to show him the pigs, but he wouldn't venture near the sties and stood back holding a hankie to his nose.

I gave the old sow a quick scratch. At least she is always there. The others disappear, like the boy calves, and then different younger ones take their places in the sties next to Sarah.

I gave her that name and it suits her. She loves being scratched with a stick and it's wonderful to hear her grunts of ecstasy as I rub. I would have gone on but Henry was looking longingly at the house, so I thought I'd better be a good hostess and lead him back indoors.

I couldn't face anything more to eat but put the kettle on and offered Henry some of Mrs Stow's newly baked scones. He tucked into four of them, with lashings of butter, and drank three cups of tea. I can't imagine how he stays so thin but he says he doesn't eat like that in London.

I phoned for a taxi after that as Henry seemed nervous about meeting August. I didn't know when he'd be home so Henry said he'd catch the 5.10 to Victoria.

I waved him away at the gate feeling quite sad. I do hope he'll come again before too long.

6

Sunday evening

When August got home yesterday he was tired and a bit dispirited. It had been a long day and he hadn't got the prices for the calves that he'd been hoping for.

When I told him Henry had been, he was awfully annoyed.

I probably shouldn't have said anything, but it's nice to talk at the end of the day — like a proper family. I always ask him what he's done and tell him about my day but as they are all so similar — visits from Mil, chats with Mrs Stow, reading and smoking — I thought Henry's visit might be of interest.

Unfortunately it wasn't. At least not the sort of interest I had intended.

'What the devil did that chap want coming down here?' said August, his eyebrows drawing together as they always do when he's angry.

His unpleasant tone made *me* angry and we had the first row we've had since being married.

'Why shouldn't he come?' I said. 'Henry's

my friend and someone I've known much longer than any of you lot down here.'

August stood in front of the kitchen table and I stood on the other side, about to get one of Mrs Stow's pies out of the oven. But August didn't sit down and I didn't reach for the oven gloves. We faced each other, both red in the face and with fists clenched.

Out of the corner of my eye I saw Wolf and Reg get up and disappear into the hall.

'I suppose he went on about missing your magnificent performances? And the girls all asking about you? And no doubt hoping that your marriage was proving a disaster and you'd soon be returning to London?'

'He didn't, actually. He was very interested in the yard and the animals and he loved the cats,' I said.

'Cats!' August snorted, then dragged his chair back from the table with a horrid scraping sound.

'And he loved Mrs Stow's cooking and came back for seconds. I think he really *envied* me my life on the farm,' I went on.

This wasn't entirely true as Henry would probably have been delighted if I'd said my marriage was a mistake and I wanted to return to London. But August had no right to assume something he knew absolutely nothing about.

My husband hadn't finished.

'Show him around, did you? Round the house and upstairs to the pink bedroom?' August sat down with a thud and his eyes were blazing. 'Did you go into our bedroom? Or did you parade in front of the double bed? Perhaps he suggested giving it a go, for old times' sake?'

This was too much. August could get his own supper and I'd come down later and get something to eat when he was sleeping. He slept so heavily he wouldn't know if I was there or not.

I slammed out of the kitchen, trod on Reg's tail, making him yelp, and stormed up the stairs.

Then I decided to sleep on the double bed for that night. It was far more comfortable than the narrow single bed I lay on beside August, and I needed SPACE.

Why is it that if you've been on the stage everyone presumes you have no morals? I don't believe that theatre folk live and love any differently to anyone else.

When I was doing *Mother Goose* in Leeds — I was still a student at Miss Griggs' — there were twelve of us dancers in that panto and eight of us were still virgins. That's not a bad percentage.

Of course we talked a lot about sex in the

dressing room, and were very interested to know who had, and who had not 'done it'. And what was it like? etc. etc. But the few who had 'done it' were not madly enthusiastic, and the girl who sat next to me — Rowena — who was a black-haired beauty with wonderful dark eyes and an amazing bosom (though not particularly good at dancing), said she didn't know what all the fuss was about.

'It's fun for the men,' she had said, leaning forward to add more mascara to her heavily lashed eyes, 'but dead boring for us, if you ask me.'

Nobody contradicted her so I believed her.

And I remember Lyn saying that when she worked as a part-time typist before coming to the Windmill, the girls in the office were devils with the men — many of whom were married — and were having affairs with most of them.

They used to boast about their activities during the tea-breaks and Lyn said it made her feel sick.

They thought she was a dark horse because she wouldn't talk about her boyfriends, and they knew she was a ballet student. But she was a virgin then and still is, to my knowledge, unless the French men have been her undoing.

I had also never been to bed with a man until I married August, but he was an ideal teacher and I quickly realized that Rowena had been quite wrong. August was gentle and patient and our honeymoon was a joyous and exciting time.

Now that we are back on the farm and living properly as man and wife, we do not make love as often as I should like, but he has no right to assume that I am having sex with Henry behind his back.

Monday afternoon

I slept very well last night in that huge bed and completely forgot that it had once been Mil's. But I'll be back with my husband tonight. There's no point in carrying on bad feelings and we were both very polite with each other this morning. It's best to try and put all those angry words behind us.

August has gone out again so I'm going to spend this time remembering the good old days then I'll concentrate on the present.

I first started dancing when Auntie came to the Home. I suppose Jane Eyre would have called her a benefactress.

She was a thin, tweedy lady who wore sensible brogues, a sensible felt hat, no make-up and a thin occasional smile. Her eyes were a very light blue and appeared lashless, and her hands were bony and long-fingered. And cold. Same sort as Mrs Dawson, I suppose, but much nicer to me.

It was Auntie who introduced me to Miss Griggs' School of Dance, and I shall always be grateful to her for opening up my austere little world at the Home.

Auntie seemed to know Matron very well, and she must have had a lot of money because she paid for my classes at Miss Griggs' until I left and began earning my own living on the stage.

I wonder if Auntie is now benefactress to some other little girl at the Home? She came to my wedding with Miss Griggs but I haven't seen her since.

Well, why should I? That was another life in London and we never talked much, anyway. She just came and escorted me across Earls Court on that first day and introduced me to Miss Griggs.

As well as paying for my classes, she also forked out for all the leotards and tights and shoes — endless pairs of shoes — flat pumps, point shoes, character shoes, and tap shoes — which changed frequently as my feet grew bigger.

After Auntie was sure I knew my way — I

didn't need a bus; it was just across Earls Court from one end to the other — Matron allowed me to go alone so long as she knew where I was going and what time I'd be back.

Schooling was pathetic. We always longed for the air raids because they wasted lots of time — so my education was only saved by the fact that I loved, and still do, reading. At the Home there was a big room at the rear, on the ground floor, where we sat on wooden chairs at wooden desks and learned the obligatory '3 Rs'.

There were only girls in the Home, about twenty on our side and the littlies on the other side with Miss Lamb. We ranged from five years old to Kathryn Jane, who was greatly admired by the rest of us and almost grown up. I wonder if she is still there helping on Miss Lamb's side? She did love the babies.

Kathryn Jane had very wavy black hair, which she tied back in a ponytail, and big, thickly lashed blue eyes. She was beautiful so maybe a man has caught her now, but she helped Matron a lot and we all adored her during my years there.

Our teacher was called Miss Laycock. She was thin and intense with no make-up, and had pale brown hair wound in a tight roll round her head. She used to come in every morning with her old dog, and teach us tables, spelling, dictation and reading aloud lessons. We also had to do a few adding up and subtracting sums, which I hated.

Two afternoons a week, until I became a full-time student, I used to go to my beloved dancing classes. None of the others came to dancing with me — I suppose they didn't have a benefactress — but when I was not dancing I had to join the bigger ones with handiwork. Kathryn Jane took the younger ones for a walk.

Handiwork was another thing I hated. We had to knit small garments for the littlies — or the newcomers, as they were called — sometimes really tiny babies came in next door. Unwanted, illegitimate, like me, unloved or orphaned. But at least there was a place for them at the Home.

Miss Lamb took care of them. I don't know why Matron didn't have a proper name — nor did Auntie — but Matron was for the bigger girls and Miss Lamb was for the littlies.

Back to the knitting.

I was wrong to say it was tiny garments. It wasn't. Well, not often. Which was a pity as they would have been quicker to make. Small babies grow and they soon outgrew all the small garments we made. So these were washed and kept for the next arrivals and more, bigger ones, were needed.

We, the older girls, knitted larger pullovers and cardigans and *those* soon wore out with all the wear and tear and washing and chewing, so more had to be produced. If we had time, we also knitted for ourselves.

Kind folk used to bring old woollen things to the Home which we had to unravel, soak in a bowl of water to get rid of the wrinkles, squeeze out and hang over the fender to dry.

Then we used to sit in pairs, facing each other, one with raised hands and the other winding the wool round and round until a skein was produced. When it was a complete skein, it had to be wound again into a tight ball.

It was all right if you liked the girl opposite and could have a reasonable conversation with her, but I usually had fat Hannah, who wasn't the least bit interested in dancing, or else Judy.

I wonder where Judy is now? She wasn't too bad — much nicer than fat Hannah — but she did cry a lot. We had all been told to be especially nice to Judy. She was a latecomer because her mum had been killed in an air raid and her dad was missing.

I really tried. But the trouble was she didn't like dancing, didn't like reading and was so miserable all the time it was difficult to know what to say to her.

Luckily, some time after she had arrived, and when it was decided (by Matron) that I should partner her whenever possible, and she had been given the bed shoved up next to mine in our bedroom, which normally slept eight and now had Judy as number nine — I discovered that she quite liked singing.

As singing was my second favourite activity after dancing, we soon drove everyone nearly mad with our renderings of 'Ten Green Bottles' and 'Clementine' and 'One and Only Youooo'. But Matron didn't stop us too often because she felt sorry for Judy and was glad she was happy doing something.

Once we had several balls of wool ready, we could begin knitting our garments. It didn't matter about colours so there were numerous Joseph's coats of many colours worn in the Home — mainly of faded browns and blues and greys.

Side to middle sheets was another chore and needed lots of singing to see us through. All our sheets became worn in the middle and as money was scarce it was a matter of 'mend and make do'.

On Matron's orders and *only* when she said — we stripped the bed/beds she told us about, cut down the middle of each sheet very carefully, they tore if you looked at them, then made a neat hem joining the two sides in the middle and hemmed the cut sides with equal care.

It was laborious and boring work even *with* the singing, and I longed to be away at my dancing. But if we wanted sheets under our rough blankets we had to persevere. Fortunately there were always Tuesdays and Thursdays to look forward to. Those were magical words — Tuesdays and Thursdays were DANCING DAYS!

Rationing for clothes didn't end until last year, when I had already left the Home, but the war years weren't too bad for us. I remember the excitement of sleeping down in the Underground, which was fun because I could make sure who I lay next to — *not* fat Hannah!

But then Matron decided it was an awful nuisance having to race down to Earls Court station every time the sirens sounded the alert — carrying babies, bottles, gas masks, etc. So she told us we should just congregate in the kitchen and classroom, and hope. Which we did, crouching under the tables and desks and praying. Luckily our street was never hit like poor Miss Griggs' first studio.

It was at one of Miss Griggs' classes in her new studio that I first met Lyn Goddard. She was older than me by a year and was tall and striking with long blonde hair and amazing legs. We quickly became friends because we got changed next to each other, and stood next to each other at the barre. We also giggled at the same things.

When Miss Griggs called out, 'You've lost your balance, Annie Brown, hurry up and find it!' I'd wobble even more and especially when I heard Lyn sniggering behind me. And when Miss Griggs told Lyn she stuck her chin out like a chicken: 'No hens in here, if you please, Miss Goddard!' we'd double up with laughter, particularly when nobody else seemed to find her words amusing.

Luckily Miss Griggs had a good sense of humour and accepted our hilarity just so long as it didn't go on for too long and disrupt the rest of the class. Which it didn't, because we loved dancing and Miss Griggs was a jolly good teacher so we passed all our exams with ease.

Lyn's home was in a large flat in South Ken and, once the war was almost over and we were winning because the Yanks had come to help us, I was allowed to go with her after class and have tea with her mother.

I suppose Mrs Goddard telephoned Matron. I don't know about that. But I do remember Lyn saying, 'Would you like to come home with me? Mum has asked Matron and it's all right by her.'

I was thrilled. It was another adventure away from the Home. We went on the Underground from Earls Court to South Ken and Lyn paid for our tickets with money from her little cloth purse. Then it was a five-minute walk from the station to the huge Victorian building where she lived.

I remember climbing lots of stairs before she opened her front door with her own key, and we entered a spacious flat.

Lyn had told me that she and her mum had moved back to London in 1943. They had been staying in Somerset with her gran after her dad was killed during the Battle of Britain. He was a pilot.

I didn't know what to say to that but Lyn said it was all right, they were fine about it now, and as her gran didn't have much room it was good to get back to London and thank goodness their flat hadn't been bombed. She also said she and her mum were much closer since Mr Goddard had died.

I liked Mrs Goddard. She was all mauve twinset and pearls and wore her fair hair in a roll like Miss Laycock. She had a lovely tea all ready for us, laid out on a table with a lace cloth. Very posh. And little lace table napkins. I'd never seen anything like that before and was very impressed.

All the china was floral and edged with gold, and we had watercress sandwiches, and meat paste sandwiches, and little currant buns, and cups of tea out of elegant floral cups with gold rims.

I remember thinking it was the best tea party I had ever had.

At the Home we had great thick earthenware mugs and thick slices of bread with margarine, and we sat on wooden benches on both sides of the long table and ate as fast as we could before the bell went. The tea was always very hot and that was our last meal until we were given *warm* milk and two biscuits at bedtime.

Tea at the Goddards was very special and I went there many times whilst I was at Miss Griggs.

* * *

As well as looking fantastic, Lyn was a very good ballet dancer, but unfortunately her height stopped her from auditioning for a ballet company.

'Aren't there any tall men doing ballet?' I asked her once. Miss Griggs, like the Home, only had female pupils.

'I suppose there are a few,' said Lyn, 'ballerinas have to have male partners for the pas de deux and for lifts. But when I'm on point it adds inches to my height and I'll be miles higher than my partner and just look silly.'

'What'll you do, then?' I asked, knowing that she loved to dance as much as I did.

'Mother says I have to finish my shorthand and typing course just in case I don't get a dancing job, or for when I'm in between stage jobs. Then I'll have to try for pantos and summer shows.'

I couldn't imagine anything worse than sitting on my bottom all day bashing away at a typewriter, and I prayed that Auntie wouldn't insist on *me* taking a Pitman course. Luckily she didn't. But once I was allowed to leave the Home, aged fifteen, I went to live with her.

She gave me the tiniest slip of a room across the hall from her huge cluttered one, and we shared the minute kitchen and lav, which was under the stairs at the back of the hall. The bath was in the kitchen, but only used once a week, and covered with a wooden board, which made an excellent surface to put things on.

Auntie's flat was in Stanhope Gardens, very close to Gloucester Road Underground, and I did *Mother Goose* panto at that time, then continued with my full-time studies at

Miss Griggs'. But more and more I longed to have a proper job and earn my own money. Apart from the few weeks when I had been away in Leeds for the panto, and had been able to pay for my own digs and meals, I was still living on Auntie's generosity and felt both guilty and restless.

I wanted my own little room, and my own gas ring on which I could cook my own meals. Well, a boiled egg or a tin of soup hotted up, with loads and loads of toast by the gas fire. That all seemed like bliss to me then. And I felt sure poor Auntie would be extremely relieved to have me out of our very tight, and shared living space.

I think Miss Griggs must have sensed my unease, or maybe Auntie had a word with her, but one day to my joy, Miss Griggs suggested that I audition for the Windmill Theatre. I was good at both modern dance and tap and, in fact, enjoyed them more than classical ballet.

'You will be worked very hard at the Mill,' said Miss Griggs, who was an old Millerette and remembered the glorious days when Mrs Henderson owned the theatre and her manager, Mr Van Damm, first introduced his non-stop variety shows to London.

I didn't care about hard work. If I was accepted it would mean a job in London and the money to pay for my own bedsit.

When I told Auntie, she wasn't sure if she liked the idea of nude ladies cavorting about on stage (nor did I at first) but Miss Griggs had the knowledge we lacked, and we trusted her judgement.

She was able to reassure us that none of the girls *had* to appear naked if she did not want to, and those that did were not allowed to *move*, and the lighting had to be subdued and artistic. The Lord Chamberlain saw to that.

'Go and see a show,' said Miss Griggs. 'Go and see for yourselves. Then, if Annie fancies working there, I'll apply for an audition for her with Mr Van Damm.'

We must have appeared an odd couple sitting there in the fourth row of the stalls, surrounded by gentlemen in City suits. Me, very young and apprehensive, accompanied by Auntie, a thin, tweedy lady with a stern face.

The theatre was only half full at that early afternoon performance, I remember, and many of the gentlemen were dozing during the conjuring and slapstick acts. The one next to me was even snoring, no doubt after his boozy lunch. But as soon as the music quickened and the girls came on, everyone woke up and took notice.

The first number was a high-kicking routine with all the girls clad — though briefly, so far as I was concerned — in tight blue leotards of satin, fishnet tights and very high heels, with nodding ostrich plumes on their heads.

The routine was very quick, very slick and *very* exhausting I learnt later, when every leg had to be raised at *exactly* the same moment, and at *exactly* the same height! But the audience always loved it.

After that opening number I had to admit that Miss Griggs had been right, and all the other dances in the programme we saw were artistically and beautifully presented. There was only one nude and I almost missed her as I was so busy watching the six dancers, who were dressed in little straw skirts and performed in a flower-filled garden.

The girls carried floral garlands in hoops which they held above their heads and swung from side to side. They also had garlands of flowers around their necks, and I only realized their breasts were bare when the flowers moved in time with the music.

Very clever and very tasteful, I thought, and by Auntie's slight smile I knew she thought so, too.

The one real nude was posed as a statue at one end of the garden, and remained so still I imagined she was made of marble. But just as the dance ended and the other girls left the stage, a spotlight lit her up for a moment and the applause thundered out, making me realize she was a live girl. Then the curtain fell.

There — now I feel better for having put all that down — but my hand is aching and my eyes are feeling scratchy, so I'm going to stop. Anyway, I can hear August taking off his boots so I'll pop the kettle on and look attentive and pleased to see him. *This* is my life now so I must try to make him happy and be a better farmer's wife from now on . . .

7

Another Monday.

No visitors, no telephone calls, no surprises. Not much has happened since last week and as Betty Folder isn't coming till Friday, and August is away for the day, and Mrs Stow has gone home, I'll carry on with my memories and write down when I first met August.

That *was* an exciting day!

* * *

It was in the January of 1948 because I had been at the Windmill for a year and the 'Windmill Girl of the Year' trophy was going to be presented in the February.

We all longed to receive that fabulous cup, but it was a total secret between Mr Van Damm and his assistant, and nobody knew the winner until her name was announced.

The cup was awarded for beauty, charm and ability, and was given to the girl whom Mr Van Damm considered had made the most improvement during the past year.

I was hopeful of winning because I had

worked extremely hard, and learnt an enormous amount since the amazing day when Miss Griggs had taken me for an audition on that famous stage.

Mr Van Damm remembered Miss Griggs, and was interested in seeing one of her pupils. Of course, I had to prove that I was good enough for that celebrated theatre, and Miss Griggs had made up a dance for me with plenty of high kicks, and some pirouettes as well, as I was good at turns.

She had informed me earlier that Mr Van Damm liked taking girls who had been classically trained. They knew how to discipline their bodies, and were better at learning choreography than girls who had only done modern dance, or tap.

Luckily he was pleased with how I looked, and how I performed, and said he would accept me at once to join the group of girls already at the Windmill.

The very next day Auntie and I went round the bedsits in Earls Court (I liked that area) and found an ideal room on the second floor of Mrs Walker's house in Barkston Gardens. So, in that January of 1947 I moved into my new room and my new job in the same week. One year later, I met August.

He and a group of friends had come up to London to see a show, and I'll never forget

Bill, our stage door keeper, bringing round a note to me in the dressing room. It was addressed to 'The pretty blonde girl on the right in the fan dance'.

How we laughed in the dressing room that night, and how envious the others were, wanting to know what I would say, and longing to know what my new admirer looked like.

His writing was very clear and neat and he just asked if I would give him the pleasure of having dinner with him after the show. He said he was a farmer and didn't often get up to town, and it would be a very special occasion for him if I would honour him with my presence.

His name was August Blake.

How could I refuse such a courteous request?

I did go up in one of our breaks (our dressing rooms were under the stage) and have a word with Bill.

'He's not old and fat with false teeth, is he?' I remember asking.

Bill shook his head. 'He looked a real gent, Honey, and was so young and handsome I reckon you'll make a fine pair. Well spoken, too. Looks a bit like Gregory Peck, he does.'

Well, Gregory Peck was my *most* favourite film star so I had to see this Mr August Blake.

'When he comes round again, tell him Miss Honey Brown will be delighted to join him for a meal,' I said.

It was a Saturday night and I wasn't in the next programme, which would be rehearsing on Sunday. Otherwise I wouldn't have been happy about getting back to my digs at goodness knows what hour, then having to be back at the theatre by nine next morning.

If it was a new show, we had the dress rehearsal at ten on Sunday mornings, and had to be in by nine to get all the make-up and hairstyles done. But that coming Sunday was a free one for me, and a welcome chance to catch up on washing and ironing and sorting out plans for the following week, so I knew I would be able to sleep late.

* * *

After the last routine had finished on that eventful night, I changed quickly but didn't remove my make-up. Just tidied my hair after removing my headpiece. Mr Van Damm could not abide untidy hair. Then I went out of the stage door and was met by this tall, broad-shouldered, gorgeous stranger.

I was completely overwhelmed as we shook hands and could not believe my luck.

I remember Bill grinning at me and giving

the thumbs up sign as I took the arm of my new admirer.

We went to a little Italian restaurant on Shaftesbury Avenue and August was so easy to talk to, and so very attentive, the hours flew by and I didn't feel a bit tired.

I had only been out with Henry before. But with Henry it had been business, as he wanted to become my agent and had great ideas for my future, so we had only talked shop.

Mr Van Damm looked after 'his girls' and we were always watched so that we came to no harm, especially when we were new at the Windmill, or very young. As I was only seventeen at that time I hadn't been out with an admirer before.

But Mr Van Damm knew Henry and he wasn't an admirer, anyway, so when August Blake turned up and Bill decided he was a bit of all right and informed Mr Van Damm accordingly, permission was given for me to go off with my farmer.

August does look like Gregory Peck, only his eyes are blue and G.P's are brown. But he's tall and dark-haired and polite, and graceful in movement, and his hands are long-fingered and beautiful, and I've never seen his nails grimy or broken.

Our meal that night was only marred by a

rather boisterous group of lads sitting at a table across from us.

'Don't mind them,' said August, moving his chair so that he had his back to them. 'We all came to the show together. We are old friends and come up to town once a year after Christmas. The others dared me to ask you out.'

I was a bit taken aback when he said this.

'So it was only a dare?'

'Because they could tell I liked you,' he said quickly. Then he leaned across the table and looked at me with his steady blue eyes, making me feel I could forgive him anything. 'And I'm glad I did because I thought you were wonderful but would never have found the courage to invite you out if they hadn't challenged me.'

A challenge sounded better than a dare and I smiled back, feeling my heart banging away against my ribs and longing to say something clever and flirtatious. But couldn't think of anything.

'Didn't any of your friends fancy one of the other girls?' I managed at last.

'I think they fancied *all* of them,' said August, 'but they weren't brave enough to ask one out.'

'It's a very small theatre — only 320 seats,' I said. This was a subject I *could* talk about.

'But they are usually full and sometimes there's a queue outside before we've even opened!'

'I'm not surprised.' August nodded his dark head. 'The show we saw tonight was excellent. I wish Mother could have seen it but she was dead set against the idea, and wanted us to go to the new Ivor Novello musical. She was shocked at the thought of naked ladies prancing about on stage. Something you would never see in one of her beloved Ivor's productions. But not such fun for us!'

'We don't prance,' I said indignantly, 'and we're not allowed to move a muscle if we are completely nude. You didn't find anything in bad taste, did you?'

'No, I didn't. In fact, Mother would be agreeably surprised if she ever came to a show — but I know she won't.'

I was glad August didn't find our performances crude or distasteful but wasn't too sure about his choice of friends, who were making quite a din.

'How do you know those chaps?' I said, jerking my head in their direction.

'Sorry about them.' He gave a wry smile. 'They're just letting their hair down after a week of hard grind. Two are friends from school days — one now lives in Bristol and the other in Chelmsford, so we only meet up when we all make the journey to London. And the other two are from home.

One is my dairyman whom I met at agricultural college, and the other is our local vet.'

August didn't have any brothers or sisters, he told me, and his father had died in 1944.

'So he never knew how the war ended but he lived in hope. How about you?' he said. 'Do you have a big family?'

I didn't want to talk about the Home and my orphaned state, but I did like him very much and knew that if we were going to see each other again, he would have to be told the truth.

Luckily he was intrigued by the unusual past of Honey Brown.

'How lucky that you had your dancing,' he said, 'and what a lovely dancer you are, Miss Brown.'

His eyes were warm with admiration and I noticed the extraordinary length of his eyelashes as he gazed across at me. His thick dark hair had a slight curl, and his lips were firm but not thin. I thought how nice it would be to be kissed by him. He was gorgeous.

'Your Auntie sounds a splendid woman,' he went on, as I remained spellbound, 'and a most intelligent and understanding lady to accompany you to the Windmill Theatre to see a show *and* to allow you to audition there.'

His words surprised me, bringing me back to my senses.

'I hadn't thought about it like that before,' I said. 'But I've always been grateful to her for introducing me to my dancing classes at Miss Griggs', and then paying for so much when I was young.'

'I'm sure Mother wouldn't have been so amenable,' he said. 'But she is very good on the farm and I suppose we all have different talents and ideas about life.'

⋆ ⋆ ⋆

After the meal, and glad to leave the bunch of his grinning comrades behind, I waited as August summoned a taxi, wondering if he would kiss me goodbye, or even invite me to some sleazy hotel in Soho for the night. He knew I was a dancer, he had seen me wearing the minimum of clothing, so why shouldn't he expect me to be an easy lay?

Fortunately, August was a gentleman, as Bill had surmised, and didn't ruin the evening for me.

'Thank you for a very happy time, Honey Brown,' he said, lifting my hand to his lips in a wonderful old-fashioned way. 'I hope you have enjoyed it as much as I have. Will you come out with me again one day?'

I gave him my address and told him to write. I really didn't think he would, and as he didn't come to London very often I couldn't see how our friendship could develop. But I liked him oh, so much, and hoped for some small miracle to occur.

Which of course it did.

* * *

Had to have a little break then for a coffee and a ciggy. August still hasn't come in so I'll go on for a bit longer now that I'm refreshed.

I didn't win the cup that year but it didn't seem so important any more as I had other matters on my mind.

Would he write to me, or not? He hadn't given me his address so there was nothing I could do except wait — and hope.

Bless him, he didn't let me down. About three weeks after our first meeting a letter arrived at my digs.

Mrs Walker always placed all her lodgers' mail on the table in the dark little entrance hall, and when I went down one morning to collect my bottle of milk, which was put next to the table legs on the linoed floor and kept beautifully cool all day long, I saw August's neat writing on the envelope. My heart raced.

At last he had written to me!

I was so excited that I quite forgot my milk and went pounding back up the stairs with his letter clutched to my bosom.

But the milk didn't matter. Nothing mattered except opening his letter and seeing what that Gregory Peck-of-a-man had to say.

I have it with me still. In fact I've kept all the letters he wrote me during that year — just over a year — we were apart.

'*As you know,*' he wrote, '*I do not have the time to travel up to town as I am much occupied on the farm. But I wondered if you would ever have the time to come down here, Miss Brown?*

If you caught a train from Victoria to Horsham, my mother would meet you at the station. She lives with me in this farmhouse, as I think I mentioned, so it would be quite proper for you to come and stay. We have a spare bedroom.

It would be nice to get to know you better, Miss Brown, and I wouldn't be working in the evenings so we would have time to talk. I look forward to hearing from you and do hope you will be able to manage a visit to Sussex.

Yours, August Blake.'

His quaint style of writing made me smile, even though my heart was beating nineteen to the dozen. 'We have a spare bedroom' — well, he didn't expect me to share with his mother, did he? But August Blake was delightfully old fashioned and I found him charming in every way. For some magical reason he found me attractive, too.

Next day I sorted out dates with our group leader, and once I was sure of the two weekends I would have free, I wrote back to August and waited again.

I wrote to him as August. I could *not* write Dear Mr Blake, and prayed that he would be less formal with me next time.

Which indeed he was.

It was Honey in his next letter, and the second weekend in March suited him and his mother well. If I caught the 2.18 from Victoria it would get me to Horsham at 3.18 and if I walked down the stairs and made for the main exit, his mother would be waiting by the barrier.

His mother, I thought, Mrs Blake. I didn't know what her first name was and wondered if I should like her? August didn't have any brothers or sisters and his mother was a widow. And they lived together. Would she be pleasant and welcoming? Or would she resent my friendship with her only son?

Golly. I was not at all sure that she would like a showgirl from the Windmill entering her son's life. August had made her out to be a determined and strong-willed lady. I hoped very much that we would get on well together during my few days in the country.

* * *

I'm stopping now and will go on tomorrow — or the next day — or the one after that. Nothing much is happening here until Betty Folder comes on Friday . . .

8

Tuesday afternoon

I'm feeling more cheerful today and memories are filling up the hours very nicely until the evening when August comes in. So I'll carry on writing and put down my first visit — seems ages ago now.

I remember catching the train easily enough at Victoria, not many people on it, and it only stopping once at East Croydon before rattling on down to Sussex. I reached Horsham bang on time.

I wasn't sure what to expect as I handed in my ticket and walked through the barrier, but immediately a small, grey-haired lady stepped forward.

'Honey Brown?' she said, and there was August's mother standing before me.

She was smaller than I had anticipated, and square. Not a bit like her tall, loping son. And her hair (no hat) though neatly styled — not permed I didn't think — was a silvery grey above bright blue eyes. Her skin was good for an elderly person and lightly tanned. No make-up, but naturally pretty.

She talked a lot and very quickly, which I thought was being nervous at meeting me, but I've since learnt that Mil always talks that way. She led the way with light footsteps (flat sensible shoes) out into the forecourt then across the road to the bus stop.

It was the Brighton bus, she told me, as we sat side by side upstairs so I could see the countryside. Apart from going up to Leeds for *Mother Goose* I had never been out of London. To my knowledge. Of course, I might have been born in the Outer Hebrides for all I know. Must have a look on my birth certificate. I presume a place name is on it? Matron gave me mine when I left the Home but I'm not sure where it is now.

Anyway, Horsham was quite a small town and we were quickly out and trundling along country roads with fields on either side. We passed through several villages in our double-decker, green and yellow bus, then, 'nearly there,' said Mil, and stood up to ring the bell overhead.

The bus stopped on the outskirts of our village, then drove off towards the Sussex Downs. When we alighted we had to walk *miles* along an empty country road with hedges on both sides. I remember thinking of all the shops and/or buildings in London where there was always something to see if one walked anywhere. Here in Sussex it was hedges and ditches with only an occasional open field.

I thanked God it wasn't raining. No shelter anywhere and I had taken special care with my hair that morning and it was looking good for August. Rain would have *ruined* it!

Luckily I had worn my 'country' shoes (they were a bit like Mil's but smarter) but I still found it a dreadful plod. Mil insisted on carrying my holdall but after a while I took it from her. It didn't seem right for an older person to have to trudge along with my bag. It wasn't heavy but a bulky shape, which banged against our legs.

As we plodded on, me grimly, Mil cheerfully, (well, she was used to it, wasn't she?) she chattered on about her son. How he had only been called up during the final years of the war, thank the Lord, and then done a year at agricultural college before coming home and taking over from her.

After her husband died she had done her best but the farm really needed a *man* on the place. She mentioned several names of people I'd never heard of so I switched off, and wished that August had met me. I would have listened to *him*.

'Of course, once petrol rationing ends I'll be able to get my car out of storage,' said Mil, 'and life will be easier but probably not healthier.' Then she glanced across at me. 'Exercise is so good for one and you keep that nice trim figure because of all the dancing you do, don't you, dear?'

I remember smiling and saying yes, but oh, how I longed for a car at that moment and good health be damned. Thinking about my figure, I'm afraid it's not quite so nice and trim now. I *must* start doing some exercise.

When we eventually reached the rough driveway on our right, Mil said, 'This is it,' and two dogs came barking down the track to meet us. But there was no sign of August. The dogs are called Wolf and Reg, and they seemed friendly enough then, although Mil kept shouting at them to get down.

As well as wearing my flat (smart) shoes, I had on plain brown trousers, and a woollen jumper (beige) under my suede jacket. I didn't mind the dogs jumping up too much because their paws weren't muddy and I felt 'farmy'.

However, I soon discovered that I was not. It's all tweeds and corduroys down here and GUMBOOTS.

I hate tweed. It's so scratchy and heavy and I would never have dreamed of wearing corduroys then. Now I'm going to stick to my comfy slacks and jumpers unless I'm invited out. Then, that awful baggy skirt and my twinset and pearls will have to do.

Not sure about the summer. I'll have to look in the box room and see what I brought with me. Doesn't matter at present — far too cold for light things.

Thank heavens clothes rationing ended last year. It was such a pain having to 'mend and make do' all the time, although at the Windmill we were lucky and the wardrobe department turned up trumps with every new show.

* * *

I suppose it will get warmer in the summer? Don't know yet. I only visited in the autumn and spring before we married. Oh yes, and that one very quick Christmas in 1948. Then we married in March this year and it's beginning to warm up now. A tiny bit.

I wonder if I can wear my snazzy matching shorts and top in turquoise with white stripes? The shorts are really short so my legs look almost as long and beautiful as Lyn's. I know I brought that outfit with me. The top is super; sleeveless with a V-neck and collar, and buttons all down the front. I wore it in Hyde Park a couple of times and got a lot of looks!

I suppose you'd call it casual-smart. I've got some high-heeled sandals to wear with it — but not here! Will these great puddles and muddy tracks ever disappear?

* * *

Anyway, back to that first visit: Mil took my holdall again and told me to follow her, and led the way round the side of the house and into the kitchen.

It was nice and warm in there (as always) with a great big shiny range, which I admired, and at the same time wondered who cleaned it. Did August's mother do all that, or was there a Mrs Mop who came in daily?

I noticed tubs of logs and coal set beside the range, and in the middle of the room a big scrubbed wooden table with four chairs set round it. There was lots of china, plates and mugs, on a wooden dresser at one side, and a sink in front of the window and another door leading out to the scullery and larder, although I didn't know where that door led then.

It was a real farmhouse kitchen and nice and cosy.

Then Mil told me to follow her up the stairs and we went up into the front bedroom. It was the pink one, with a matching basin and striped satin chair, and a striped pink coverlet on the double bed.

'I've given you this room as it's more comfortable and warmer, being over the kitchen,' she said. 'I've left some hangers for you in the wardrobe so sort yourself out and come down for tea when you're ready. There's a lavatory for you at the end of this passage, and a bathroom at the end of the other corridor. Turn left on the landing and it's at the end there.'

I unpacked and put my extra pair of trousers and my other pullover in the cupboard next to Mil's clothes. This was really her bedroom — so where would she be sleeping that night? How odd to have that large double bed to herself. I supposed it was the one she had shared with her husband. I hoped he had liked pink. Even the wallpaper was striped in different shades of rose. And why hadn't I been given the spare room? Was she scared I would pop into her son's bed the moment she disappeared for the night?

I had very little to unpack and didn't want to go to the lav but I did want to see August. Where was he? It would have been so nice if he had been there to greet me — like his dogs. Waiting for me to arrive, expectant and welcoming. But he was nowhere to be seen.

Sticking my head out into the corridor I

saw the door to the lavatory at the very end but there was also a door further down on the left. I wondered if that was August's room. Tiptoeing down I tried the latch (very quietly because it was metal) but the room was only a dumping ground. It could once have been a spare room but was very small and crammed with cardboard boxes and suitcases.

Carefully closing the door behind me and feeling like a burglar, I padded down to the landing. There I saw the other passage running back, parallel to mine, with two doors on the right and another at the far end.

I ventured down to have a look at the bathroom, but it was all a bit creepy and cold and SILENT up there, so I scuttled back to the stairs and went down to the nice warm kitchen.

'In here!' called a voice behind me.

I turned round and walked past the stairs and the grandfather clock, and several sagging chairs and a sofa, and went into a big sitting room. Two windows looked out onto a little square of grass, and a fence and a gate, then onto a yard and some outbuildings. It wasn't a very attractive view to have from one's sitting room, I thought then, but have got used to it now. We don't often sit in there, anyway.

Mil was perched on the end of a

chintz-covered sofa with a small table in front of her on which was set a tea pot, floral, three cups and saucers, floral, and a jug and sugar bowl, also floral.

Next to the table was a trolley with tea plates, serviettes and lots of silver spoons and little forks, and plates of sandwiches and biscuits and, on the lower shelf was a *large iced cake*! I could not believe my eyes. This was better than any tea I had had at Mrs Goddard's.

I began to feel better immediately. I do love food and was beginning to feel pretty peckish by then.

'Sit there, dear,' said Mil, nodding at one of the chintz-covered armchairs.

I perched on the end, like her, and tried to look casually elegant.

'Where is August?' I said.

I remember feeling suddenly nervous. After all, I had only met him once before and that was after a performance, and I had been all dolled up and terribly excited about my first rendezvous with an admirer. And the other girls had been excited for me and wanting to know all about Mr August Blake.

I had been the centre of attention both that night and the next day when they had asked all about our meal, and what he had said to me, and what I had said to him, and had he kissed me? Etc. etc.

Then I had written to him twice and he had ditto-ed me and that was it.

I really didn't know the man and suddenly I was sitting opposite his mother in an old farmhouse, and trying to look intelligent. I wanted August to come in and make me feel attractive and important once more, and he was nowhere about.

'He'll be in any moment now,' said his mother. 'I expect he's been helping out in the dairy. We've just had a milking parlour installed, and the men are very involved with the workings and getting the cows used to it.'

It was as if she was speaking another language. How could I answer that? What was a milking parlour, anyway?

I thought it sounded like a place I'd seen once in an American film with everyone sitting on high stools at a curving bar, drinking long frothy drinks out of glasses, with straws. There was so much to learn but I wanted to hear it from August, not his mother.

'What did you have before the milking parlour?' I asked. I had to say something, so I raised my eyebrows questioningly, sipping at my tea in its floral cup. No gold rims like at Mrs Goddard's.

I far preferred coffee and was dying for a

ciggy. I had brought two packs of Peter Stuyvesant with me but didn't know if smoking was allowed. There were no ash trays in sight and although I had smoked after the meal with August that Saturday night, he had not lit up. He hadn't said anything negative about it, though.

I remember chewing on a meat paste sandwich and longing for a great chunk of iced cake. It would have taken away my craving for a ciggy.

At the Home we had Marmite and, very occasionally, meat or fish paste. And we were allowed jam on Sundays. But we never ever had an iced cake. Not even at Mrs Goddard's. I really desired that cake but apparently we had to wait for August.

Suddenly there was uproar outside, loads of hysterical barking. Mil put down her cup and smiled.

'That will be him now,' she said. 'The dogs always give him such a welcome you'd think he'd been away for days. They are not allowed in the milking parlour,' she ended.

I nodded and smiled back but my heart was thumping.

I didn't know what to do. Should I rise and offer my hand like Queen Elizabeth? Run and fling my arms around him? Give a coy smile and peck his cheek? I really didn't know and felt such a stranger.

We seemed to wait for ages for him to wash and brush up, then eventually he came through from the kitchen, his hands still a bit red and damp. Oh, what a gorgeous man, I thought again. Gregory Peck — eat your heart out!

My heartbeat quickened and I stood up and went towards him.

'Oh, August, how lovely to see you again,' I said.

He smiled and held out his arms, and I ran into them and felt *his* heart thundering against my cheek. He is very tall and in my low heels I only came up to his chest. But it felt as if I had come home.

'How was the journey?' he asked, as we slowly parted and he escorted me back to my chair.

'Fine,' I said. 'And your mother was there to meet me. It's lovely being here, August.'

I wished I didn't keep saying 'lovely' but no sensible words came out of my grinning mouth. I just wanted to stare and sit very close and hold his hand.

Which I couldn't. At least I could smile at him, and stare, but not sit close, as he was on the other armchair opposite me, and his mother was in between us on the sofa.

* * *

That evening on the farm was another experience.

The girls became quite hysterical when I told them later.

I mean there was I, a (reasonably) attractive young woman madly interested in (I won't say in love with — not then — though I probably already was) a (definitely) handsome young man, and both of us longing to get to know each other better.

I don't mean making passionate love (although that thought had crossed my mind even though I knew it would be wrong). I don't know what was in August's mind, but we had seen so little of each other — living in two different worlds — we needed this weekend to talk, and kiss, and touch, and discover what we felt about each other. We needed physical contact.

Instead, we sat all evening with Mil for company, playing three-handed Whist at the kitchen table.

The girls couldn't believe it.

'Honey, you didn't!'

'What, *all* evening?'

'Then we took it in turns to go upstairs to the bathroom,' I told them, 'and get ready for bed.'

I thought Lyn was going to fall off her chair she was laughing so much.

'We go to bed early here in the country,' I remember Mil saying. 'August has to be up at five for the milking, and I like to make him a nice bowl of porridge before he goes out.'

I stared at her. FIVE O'CLOCK?

'You needn't rise with the lark, dear,' she went on, seeing my expression. 'I'll bring you in a cup of tea at half-past seven. Will that be all right? Then we'll have breakfast at 8 when August comes in.'

I didn't know what to say. Life in the countryside was certainly different.

Nine o'clock was chiming in the hall as Mil gathered up the cards.

'Right, time for bed,' she said. 'You go first, dear. There'll be plenty of hot water if you want a bath, and it will warm you up. There's no heating in the bedrooms but yours is right over the kitchen so you'll be fine. Have a bath, dear, and then you'll pop into bed as warm as toast. You brought a dressing gown, didn't you?'

I wondered if she thought I was going to creep naked down that icy corridor. And there was no mention of Honey now. It was just 'dear', all the time.

'I'll bring you up a mug of warm milk once

you're in bed, shall I? Would you like that, dear?'

'Dear' most certainly would not. Hot milk reminded her of the Home, with two dry biscuits. She wouldn't have minded another chunk of that iced cake, though.

'No milk for me,' I said quickly. 'I've done very well this evening, thank you.'

And we had eaten well. Bowls of excellent home-made soup before our Whist, with crisp brown rolls warmed in the oven, and a dish of butter in the middle of the table so we could help ourselves. Plus an interesting milk pudding. Not rice. I couldn't have *borne* that — but something brown and creamy with apples. It tasted jolly good and I could tell there were always going to be loads of milky things on the farm every day.

As I stood up, August did likewise and walked round the table to take me in his arms.

'Night, Honey,' he whispered into my hair. 'So glad you came. I'll show you round the farm tomorrow. Make sure you are wearing suitable clothes. Did you bring boots?'

He kissed the top of my head then stood back to look down at me.

'I don't have any gumboots,' I said. 'Won't my flat walking shoes do?'

He laughed. 'Not in our mud.'

'You could borrow a pair of mine,' said Mil. 'What size are you, dear?'

'Five,' I said.

She grimaced. 'Mine will be too small — only a four, you see.'

'I'll phone Jim,' said August. 'Perhaps Betty's are a five and he could bring a pair of hers up tomorrow.'

'I don't want to be a nuisance,' I said, knowing that I was.

I didn't like the idea of wearing someone else's smelly boots but what would I be doing with a pair of gumboots in London?

Fur boots, I had. Though I hadn't brought them with me. Not with their smart little heels and lovely shiny leather almost up to my knees. They were new and had cost a pretty penny and I would *never* have considered wearing them in all the mud and what-have-you in the Sussex countryside. They had also taken the last of my coupons for that month and I wouldn't have worn them on the farm, not even to impress August.

'Good idea,' said Mil, opening the kitchen door and willing me to go upstairs. 'Off you go, then, dear. I'll see you tomorrow with a cup of tea.'

Dear had a nice hot bath — a really boiling one — after trailing down the freezing passage with pyjamas and towel and dressing-gown. The bitter bathroom warmed up nicely with hot water gushing out of the huge wide-mouthed tap, which had once been silver but was now coated with a hard green crust.

I didn't know what to do with my damp towel. There was one nail on the wall which already had a towel on it, so I hung the bath mat neatly back over the side of the bath (as we did at the Home every Saturday), left the door open behind me to let out the muggy air, remembered to switch off the light (save electricity — Matron) and plodded back down the passage.

Their two doors were still shut so they hadn't come up yet, I noticed, perhaps they were discussing me! Then I went round to my side of the house and the large pink bedroom with the double bed.

It was only after I had hung my towel over the pink hand basin — there was nowhere else to leave it — and climbed into bed that I heard their voices and footsteps coming up the stairs. Dear was safely tucked away out of sight so August could come up to bed, with his mother close behind him.

* * *

I slept surprisingly well going to bed so early — am getting used to it now! — and found the big double bed very comfortable with lots of space to spread out. But I do remember waking several times during that night, aware of odd noises.

In London there was always noise — the reassuring drone of distant traffic, and voices, and footsteps, and car doors banging, But here on the farm there was total silence. It was eerie. Then suddenly a screech, or rustle, or thud, would disturb me. I didn't know if they were dogs, or owls, or mice, but muttered a verse from the Litany just to keep myself safe. It was also pitch dark.

> '*From ghosties and whosties*
> *And long-leggedy beasties*
> *And things that go bump in the night,*
> *Good Lord, deliver us.*'

Those are my very first memories of the farm — more tomorrow, no doubt, until something exciting happens (?) . . .

9

Wednesday afternoon

Today I'm going to write down something PRIVATE. It'll be all right because no one's going to read this — it's a personal and private book for me to put down my thoughts about people and events as they come along. I do not like Dairyman Nick.

He's got insolent eyes.

I don't like the way he looks at me, I don't like what he's thinking, and I don't like HIM.

But August couldn't manage without him and he's a very good man with the cows, says Mil. So here I am, opening my heart to my diary. I'm almost on the last page I see. Bother. I'll have to get hold of another exercise book, but how?

I could ask Mil to get one for me but then she'll want to know what on earth for, and this is my secret.

I'm also longing for a new book to read.

I think Mr Blake must have been the reader in this house. Mil hasn't taken any with her and August doesn't have time. Except on honeymoon and then it was fact, not fiction.

In the cold formal dining room which we never use, there are shelves of leather-bound books and amongst them I've seen a set of Charles Dickens, the Bronte sisters and good old Jane Austen.

I asked August if I could borrow them and he said, yes, of course, but they are rather special and I'm scared of dropping coffee on one, or ash, or something dreadful. I'm also finding that a little goes a long way. I mean I *will* read my way through the classics in time (Matron and Auntie would be proud of me! And Miss Laycock) but I would like something a bit lighter in between.

I must get a bike soon. I'll learn to ride it up and down this driveway and then I'll be independent. I'll go down to the village and back on my own, and get some books from the funny little library which is a room above the chemist's shop.

Up till now I've asked Mil to choose one for me — just to break the monotony of CULTURE — then she sends it up with Mrs Stow on her bike.

I'm reading so quickly I really need more than one at a time. But if I ask for more it takes even longer for Mil to choose, and they are heavy for Mrs Stow's wobbly basket, and the ones I *do* get are not always the right ones. I want to choose my own.

I need a bike! Must badger August a bit more if he's not too tired tonight.

* * *

I wonder what Christmas is like down here. I'll ask for books then — and for my birthday in November — lots of them.

Of course, I did come that one Christmas — I'd almost forgotten but it wasn't as if I was living down here then. It was the 1948 one, when I'd met August that January, but it was such a rush with me dancing on Christmas Eve, then getting away early because I had to catch the train from Victoria — and kind Jenny taking my place for the last three routines. And then I had to be back on Boxing Day at the Windmill.

All I do remember is a very large tree in the hall — all sparkly and glittery with a few wrapped presents on the floor beneath it. I got woollen gloves from August — PINK! — which I'm sure Mil had knitted, and a scarf from her, also knitted and pink.

The dogs kept sniffing around and being shouted at, and some people I didn't know were singing outside then invited in for drinks and home-made mince pies (quite nice). They were carol singers. And all I wanted — apart from the drink and pies — was to kick off my shoes and get into my comfy dressing gown and cuddle close to August.

Mil spent hours in the kitchen on Christmas Day, roasting a goose, I think it was, and I sort of hovered, not knowing what to do. I longed to be with August but it was raining — hopeless for my hair — and he was hours outside sorting out the animals and the cows that had to be milked, etc. etc.

Speaking of cows, back to the dairyman.

I did meet him on that Sunday when I came down to Sussex for the first time. August wanted to show me the new milking parlour — he's very proud of it — and Nick was bringing the cows in when we went across before tea.

I hardly noticed him then, being so taken up with August, but we were introduced over the back of a cow and I saw a fair-haired chap, with a tanned, good-looking face, and brown eyes. He had nice white teeth, I remember, and seemed civil enough but we didn't stay long and August led me out into the yard again and on to the pigsties.

I was wearing Betty Folder's gumboots, which had been delivered and fitted well but I had to get used to their weight. Clomp, clomp. I certainly needed them in all that mud and slush and was thankful I hadn't ventured out in my (smart) 'farmy' shoes!

* * *

This morning I had my first proper encounter with that Nick.

He was crossing the yard with two dead rabbits dangling from his hand. The dogs had gone off somewhere with August, but two of the cats were very interested in what Nick was carrying and were running along beside him. I think blood was dripping from the beasts' mouths and ears, or something disgusting.

Anyway, I felt sick and turned away. I had been meaning to go down to the wood and see if my hedgehog was around, but decided to go back inside until the dairyman had disappeared.

What was he doing up here by the house? Milking was over and his cottage was away on the other side of the farm.

'Mrs Honey?' he called, before I could get away. 'I've brought you your supper.'

As I turned back to face him, he swung the poor lifeless creatures to and fro. 'Your husband likes rabbit stew,' he said. 'Here.' And he came up close and thrust the furry bodies at me.

I stepped back without looking at his offering.

'Go round and leave them in the scullery,' I

said. 'Mrs Stow can deal with them.'

'You'd best watch her skin them,' he said, staring at me with his insolent eyes. 'All farmers' wives know how to do that. Mrs Blake is a dab hand at it, you know.'

I didn't care what Mil or Mrs Stow did with those damned rabbits. I knew *I* was not going to touch them.

'Leave them,' I said again, then squelched away across the yard and went to the gate which led out to the field.

I dislike him so much. Can't explain why except that he reminds me of a stage-hand we once had at the Windmill. *He* never did anything nasty, he never *said* anything unpleasant, but he had the same sort of insolent stare and the girls didn't like him anywhere near them. This was difficult because of so many quick changes and us standing around in the wings waiting to go on.

But he made us feel so uncomfortable that our leader had a word with Mr Van Damm. He really cared about us, and one day the man wasn't there any more; a much nicer chap had taken his place. We all heaved a sigh of relief.

Now, I feel the same about this Dairyman Nick but there's no Mr Van Damm to help me on the farm. I don't want anything to do with him and wish he would keep away from me, and the house. I'll try and speak to August about him but I'll have to be ever so tactful.

Trouble is, this Nick seems to be liked by everyone except me. I am very conscious of being new here, and pretty useless — except in bed! But that time spent with my husband is so *short* when compared with the hours and hours he spends outside.

However, there is something I can do that August really likes and only *I* can do. And I hold it to my heart and am comforted by the knowledge because old Snake-Eyes can't do it, nor fussing adoring Mil, nor Oh-so-good-with-the-cows, nice white teeth and blond curls Mr Dairyman Nick.

I can wear stockings and a suspender belt, high heels and a saucy bra, and August likes sitting on the bed and watching me parade in front of him.

He likes it when I take off all my clothes — keeping my high heels on — then use a bath towel which I hold up at the corners and use like the ostrich-feather fans we had at the Windmill. But luckily the towel is *much* lighter! He likes me to dance and move with the towel, hiding and teasing with my body, just the way I did when he first saw me. Only then he couldn't touch me because the footlights were in the way.

Now he can do anything he likes with me and what happens next is NOT for this diary — private though it is. But it makes us both happy and it's the only time my husband really belongs to me.

Such a short length of time; such very precious moments.

I do have to judge it carefully, though. The timing has to be right. August gets very tired and after a long day, especially if things haven't gone well — like at the market, or the milk yield is down, or too many boy calves — he can be very depressed and doesn't want to make love.

But I am learning about my husband and getting better at judging his moods, and I know some time the evening will be right for me to seduce him . . . It is just a matter of patience . . .

Thursday afternoon

This morning I had more problems with that wretched Nick.

I had gone out to pick some forsythia. Mrs Stow had told me its name and as the daffodils are over now, I thought the forsythia would make a lovely splash of colour in the hall. I thought I'd arrange it in Matron's blue/white/yellow vase on the little windowsill so it looks bright and cheerful there all day and evening.

Nature is amazing — the flowers come out before the leaves!

And while I'm at it — about Nature, I mean — the hedges are all gloriously covered with white — bright green with white blossom threading through and dancing along the top, and fairly bursting out every few feet, or so.

It seemed to happen quite suddenly, almost overnight. No wonder Robert Browning wrote, 'Oh, to be in England now that April's there'. Spring has well and truly sprung. It's hawthorn blossom, Mrs Stow says, and it looks Fan-Tab-U-Lous! We didn't have *that* in London.

* * *

I felt really cheerful walking back to have my coffee and chat with Mrs Stow, my hands full of forsythia, when I saw two rabbit skins stretched out and nailed onto a plank beside the back door.

They were in full sun and didn't have heads or feet so I could bear to look at them. I supposed they were drying out in the sun

— but whatever for? Mrs Stow had obviously skinned them so that meant we'd be having rabbit stew, or pie, for lunch. Yuk. *Not* my most favourite dish.

Feeling less cheerful, I entered the kitchen to find Dairyman Nick in there. He was standing very close to Mrs Stow at the sink, and they both had their backs to me. Mrs Stow was giggling and saying, 'Oh, you are wicked, Mr Nick!' in a silly girly voice, and he had one arm around her ample waist and was attempting to kiss her cheek.

My stomach heaved at the sight and I turned round to leave the room when he saw me.

'It's the beautiful Mrs Honey!' he called out. 'Good morning to you. Come for your morning gossip, have you?'

Mrs Stow tutted and pulled away from him and wiped her hands on a cloth lying on the draining board.

'Come in and don't mind him,' she said. 'He's just come for the rabbit.'

Whilst she marched away into the scullery, Nick leaned his back against the sink and stared at me, folding his arms across his chest.

He is tall and lean and remarkably good-looking with his blond hair and brown eyes, and I dislike him intensely.

I didn't speak but was not going to look away so returned his stare, still clutching my forsythia, until Mrs Stow came back with a bowl in her hands, covered with a white cloth.

'Here you are then, Mr Nick. Pop it in the oven with an onion and some carrots and it'll keep you going for a day or two.'

'What? None of your good pastry, Mrs Stow? No rabbit pie for me today, then?'

She glanced quickly at me before shaking her head and giving him a little push towards the door.

'Off with you now, and no more of your cheek, Mr Nick,' she said briskly. 'Leave us in peace.'

He took the pot from her then sauntered out of the kitchen.

Presumably he had no wife. Pity. I would feel safer and stronger if he had a woman living with him in that cottage. I wonder if Mrs Stow often cooks for him. Perhaps Mil didn't like it and that explained her rather furtive glance at me.

'What are those rabbit skins doing outside?' I said, going across to collect my vase from the cupboard.

I didn't intend encouraging any cooking for that man. What if he started coming in for meals with August? Or joined me when August was away somewhere? What a frightful thought. How could I deal with that?

'I'm going to make mittens,' said Mrs Stow. 'Lovely warm mittens for Mrs Folder's little Jerry. You should watch next time I skin them, duck. It's a useful knack, and Mr Nick is often catching them beasts with his ferrets.'

'I don't think so, Mrs Stow,' I said, filling the vase and arranging my branches of forsythia. 'Let's have tea and then I've got some letters to write.'

I didn't have any letters, and I had run out of Nescafé so was in a bad mood. But I was glad to leave the kitchen after a short chat and a ciggy, place my vase on the windowsill, and go and read another chapter of *Bleak House*.

10

Friday evening

Betty came up this afternoon, which cheered me enormously.

Jerry was strapped to her back, and after tethering Randy on one side of our driveway so he could munch happily away, she came into the kitchen for a cup of tea and a natter.

She doesn't smoke so I try not to when she and Jerry are there. He is crawling everywhere now so we shut the doors into the hall and into the scullery, and allowed him to explore the kitchen.

I opened one of the lower cupboard doors where some pans are kept, and he had a wonderful time pulling them out, and their lids, with noisy abandon.

Betty and I had to shout a bit but we got used to the din and she wanted to know all about my dancing. It was great to 'talk shop' again and she genuinely wanted to know.

'Why is it called the Windmill?' she asked.

'Because there was a *real* mill there in the reign of Charles II. Can you imagine it? All fields and bushes — like this farm — right in the middle of London!'

'What's it like inside? Is it a big theatre?'

'Not the auditorium, but the whole building is fairly large and there's lots going on in it.'

'Tell me,' she said, her eyes bright with anticipation. 'Tell me about your world.'

'Our dressing rooms are underneath the stage but if you climb the stairs we've got a big rehearsal room with huge mirrors on the walls, so we can see ourselves from every angle.'

Betty blushed. 'Isn't it embarrassing looking at all those pink bodies?'

'But we aren't *nude*!' I said. 'We aren't allowed to dance with no clothes on. The real nudes have to keep as still as statues.'

'Oh,' she said.

'Sometimes our draperies are a bit transparent, or don't exactly cover everything,' I admitted, 'but it's only our breasts which sometimes show — never anything below the waist.'

I described the fan dance and said how we all longed to be the main dancer. She *was* completely naked but moved her fan so skilfully that her body was never seen by the audience. She was also assisted by her companions, one of whom was me, and we had to make sure we covered all her actions with our own fans whenever hers left her body for a moment. The Lord Chamberlain was very strict about *that*.

'By golly, we had to practise,' I said, remembering all the tension and concentration with a whoosh of excitement, 'because timing was absolutely essential and those ostrich plumes were jolly heavy. We had to train for weeks to get that performance right.'

'What about food?' said plump Betty. 'Did you take sandwiches? Or pop out for a snack? You must have been starving after all that dancing.'

'We were,' I said. 'But there's a kitchen upstairs, and a canteen, so we all ate there. We had a wardrobe department, as well, for all our costumes. It really was a little world of our own. There was even a lift to go up to the top floors, but that was for Mr Van Damm and the office staff.'

'Don't you miss it, Honey?' said Betty.

'A bit,' I said. In fact, I missed the theatre world more than I was willing to confess. But it was super having Betty there, asking questions, and wanting to know so much about my past.

'Show me,' she said suddenly, sitting forward. 'Not the naughty bits but the ballet you learnt at dancing school.'

'All right,' I said. It had been ages since I

had danced and now was my chance to show off.

We pushed back the kitchen table then found that if we put it on its side in one corner, and opened the lower doors of two cupboards on either side, it made a splendid den for Jerry and kept him safe.

Betty leaned back against the dresser and clapped her hands.

'Now for some ballet,' she said.

I pirouetted across the floor and she oohed and aahed and Jerry shouted from his cage.

An audience again! Honey Brown was in her element.

There wasn't much space but I leapt across from one corner to the other, doing grande jetés, then ran round to posé forward and end in an arabesque followed by a neat (nearly) fifth position of my feet. Panting.

Betty was thrilled. 'Let me try something,' she said.

'I'll give you a lesson but I'm not sure about those jodhpurs,' I said. 'Why don't you take them off?'

She went bright red.

'Then I'd just be in my knickers! I've got to cover myself, Honey. Somebody might come in!'

I raced upstairs and collected my revolting full skirt and carried it down for her. She slipped out of her riding gear and pulled on my skirt which had an easy waist band and fitted her reasonably well. At least she was freer in that and her modesty remained intact.

'My legs will be fine for ballet,' she announced cheerfully, 'I've got good strong thighs thanks to my riding.'

I wasn't too sure about her good strong thighs, but gave her the back of a chair to hold on to.

'That's your barre,' I said. 'Hold on with one hand and allow the other to hang gracefully by your side.'

I faced her, doing exactly the same, holding on to another chair back.

'First we do pliés,' I said, 'to warm our muscles up.' And demonstrated, feet apart, toes out, back straight. 'Look ahead as you bend your knees slowly over your feet.'

Oh dear, it was a disaster.

Betty's bottom stuck out, her knees fell forward, and her top half sagged.

'Betty, stand up straight — look at me!' I said, showing her again. But it was no use. She had no idea how to control her body and began to giggle.

Then I giggled, and little Jerry began to chuckle so loudly that he sat down on his heavily nappied bottom with a THUMP.

'I don't think I was meant to be a ballerina,' cried Betty, collapsing over her chair back.

'You need training,' I gasped, wiping my eyes. 'You need years and years of classes. But I didn't realize simple pliés could be so difficult!'

I showed her a few leg movements after that, like grande battement and ronde-de-jambe, but we got even more hysterical trying these together and finally decided to stop before she did herself an injury.

Jerry was on his feet by then, hanging on to the upturned legs of the table and upping and downing his fat little body, like a Jack-in-the-box.

'You should give dancing classes in the village, Honey,' said Betty, once she had recovered her breath. 'For adults as well as children. There isn't a dancing school any closer than Horsham and I'm sure lots of mums would like to get their figures back after having a baby. And children love to dance. I know several in the village who would like to learn, and Jerry, too.' She grinned at her son.

'Wait a minute,' I said, going to fill the kettle at the sink. 'I haven't yet learnt how to be a good farmer's wife.'

'But farming isn't really you, is it?' she said.

'And dancing is. You should stick to what you do best, Honey.'

I'm afraid that remark annoyed me.

'Are you saying I'm not a good wife to August?'

'I'm not saying that at all,' said Betty, struggling to get back into her jodhpurs. 'Don't get ratty. All I'm saying is do something you really *enjoy* and it will bring you in some money of your own, as well.'

That calmed me. Money would be very, very useful. Earned by me, to do with exactly what I pleased.

'I've never done any teaching,' I said, placing the kettle on the hob. 'Once you've been on the stage, teaching seems rather tame.'

'Well, think about it,' said Betty, decently clad once more and placing my skirt carefully folded on a spare chair.

And I will. But I wonder what August will say to that idea? A working wife? Hmm. I don't think he'll like it. And Mil? Now *she* might think it a good idea — being such an accomplished and industrious lady, herself.

'We'd better go and release my son before he starts hollering,' said Betty.

So we went across to stand the table on its legs again and let Jerry out of his cage, then sat down with our tea and some of Mrs

Stow's scones, and talked of other things.

It was lovely seeing them and I intend asking them again soon. Betty is the first real friend I've made down here, but I'd probably make more if I started classes in the village.

* * *

One other nice thing happened today. I heard the cuckoo early in the morning.

I have never heard one before — only read about it in books — and I was so excited: I heard it out of the bedroom window as I was making the beds, and I rushed downstairs to tell Mrs Stow.

But she wasn't a bit impressed.

'Nasty cruel things,' she said. 'They come over from foreign parts and take over our birds' nests, then throw out all the eggs and put their *own* in.'

'I didn't know that,' I said. 'Why do they do it?'

Mrs Stow shrugged. 'Dunno — always have. Then our little birds feed their great fat chick and look after it until it flies away. And good riddance, I say, till next year comes and it all happens again.'

I'll have to ask Mil to get me a book on birds from the library and I'll find out more. It's a shame, really, because the cuckoo's call sounds so romantic and is a sure sign that spring is here.

I suppose it's a bit like Dairyman Nick; nice on the outside but bad within. Of course I don't know what a cuckoo looks like but the sound it makes is lovely and haunting. And Nick may *look* handsome but there is something unpleasant about him. I just wish somebody else would think the same as me.

Ah, that's August taking off his boots — I'll stop now and carry on another day . . .

11

Tuesday

I've got a bicycle! I am so excited and am practising hard up and down the driveway. I've never ridden one before. Why should one need a bike in Earls Court with the Underground just round the corner?

I almost achieved success today.

I wait until the afternoon and have a go once Mrs Stow has gone home and milking is in progress. Then it's safe.

Although I am used to audiences I do not intend making a fool of myself and intend being both confident and graceful before being seen by anyone.

Just a few more rehearsals and then I'll be brave enough to go down to the village.

It was Old Stow's idea. He is Mrs Stow's husband and looks after the chickens and the vegetable garden.

August brought it up on the back of his truck on Saturday. I don't know how much he paid for it and hope it wasn't too expensive, but a mate of Old Stow's was selling his daughter's. She's got married and is expecting and doesn't want it any more, apparently. So Old Stow got it all polished up and put on new tyres, then gave it to August. And I love it!

Old Stow is going to show me how to mend a puncture. There's an interesting little tin in a bag behind the saddle, and I believe one has to do something with a bucket of water and glue? Something like that.

Anyway, parts of the metal have been painted blue — Old Stow says it wasn't him — but it looks great (thank heavens it isn't pink:) and I'm going to call it SKY.

It will make life so much easier if I can go into the village whenever I want. I hate asking Mil, or Mrs Stow, to get things for me. There is no *privacy* in shopping.

I might even be able to get into Horsham if I hide my bike behind the hedge by the bus stop. Must ask Old Stow if he can get a padlock and chain for me. He's always called Old Stow — don't know why.

But money is the problem. I don't have a penny of my own, except for a bit I saved in my post office savings book, and I don't want to use that. It's for a rainy day, as Matron used to say. And I don't know where it is. I'm sure I brought it with me — must look.

I suppose the name and address will have to be changed before I can use it, anyway.

Signature is different, too. Now I am Honey Blake but on the savings book I was Annie Brown. Shall I make it Annie Blake? That is my proper name and I'm always called Annie by Auntie and Matron and Miss Griggs.

But Honey was my stage name and I think it's nicer than Annie. So I shall be Honey Blake on everything I sign from now on.

I wonder what's on my marriage certificate? Isn't it awful — I don't know! It all happened so quickly with August proposing and me accepting, then Mil organizing everything down here and me dancing all the time. Then all that business in church and having to meet the vicar beforehand and telling him I would love and obey August always.

I did say that to the vicar, and in church in front of all those people, and before God, but I'm not sure if I will. Love him, yes, of course, but obey?

I mean what if he tells me to do something awful? He wouldn't — not August — I mean nothing illegal or wicked. But he might ask me to do something I really, really don't want to do. Like invite that Dairyman Nick for a meal. I would rather DIE.

August doesn't know how much I dislike that man. It's not the sort of thing we can discuss easily and anyway, when do we sit down and have a good chin-wag? It's always rush, rush, rush, with him.

Out of bed, out of the house, in for breakfast, out again, in for lunch (sometimes), out again, in for supper (usually), then a final out, then home and into the bathroom — bed.

Oh yes, and at nine o'clock — always — the news on the wireless before going upstairs.

August doesn't get a newspaper — only the *Farmers' Weekly* — but the nine o'clock news is an absolute *must* and no talking whilst it is on.

We don't even talk in bed. If I'm lucky I can get him interested and seduce him — but more often than not he's asleep before I've kissed him goodnight.

Such a long heavy body — but really relaxed in bed — that's why he needs one to himself. Mine is pushed up close, right up beside his so we can reach out and touch each other if we want. But we don't. In separate beds, and on separate mattresses, and with our own blankets, we don't disturb each other if we toss and turn.

Which I do a lot but August never stirs.

Sometimes I wonder if he is still alive and sit up in a fright and lean across to listen and make sure he's breathing. He always is.

He doesn't snore (thank God) so there's no way of knowing if he's all right unless I listen. Then I can lie down again in relief and try to sleep myself.

When we have little July it will be lovely because I'll have it beside me. I don't mean in my bed — in a Moses basket on the floor beside me. And when it's bigger it'll go into the cot next door and I'll be able to pop round and check on it every time I check on August.

Come on, Honey, have a baby soon . . .

* * *

I was getting a bit morose just then so, to cheer myself up, I went and had a look at my wedding dress.

It hangs on one side of the big cupboard in the pink bedroom covered with an old sheet. Mil must have put it there and this afternoon I got it out, uncovered it and held it against me as I looked in the mirror.

I didn't put it on — just looked — remembering when August proposed and Mil told me to try on *her* wedding gown.

I didn't like the idea at all but couldn't tell her that, so when she came in with it over her arm and said, 'Try it on, dear, and see,' I had to.

And by golly, I fell in love with it immediately. It's gorgeous — of cream-coloured silk — very 1920s and very glam. It's got long floating sleeves, a round-necked bodice which falls to a dropped waistline, and soft panels of silk to the ankles.

It fitted me like a glove. I couldn't believe it: Mil must have been a lot slimmer in her youth, and I suppose my legs showed more than hers as I'm a bit taller, but my legs are good so that didn't bother me.

She had even kept the little cream roses (artificial) which were clipped on either side of the headband, and the long lace veil, all of which I wore. But her white satin shoes were too small so I managed to buy a pair of size fives when I went back to town.

And I remembered August taking me into Horsham on that Saturday afternoon and us choosing an engagement ring together. It's not a diamond but a square-cut ruby. I don't wear it very often but it lies in its velvet-lined box in the top drawer of my dressing table and I often get it out and stroke it and feel happy just looking at it.

Like the wedding dress, that ring brings back wonderful memories of our week in Wales. I wore it every day then, on top of my wedding ring. What magical days those were — really the only time we have been completely alone together for days on end. Bliss.

After I'd hung the dress carefully back in the cupboard, I came down again to finish this — next time I've got to search for my savings book. Until I find it I have to ask August for pocket money and it's really embarrassing. I wish he'd give me a regular amount of my own. I suppose a housekeeping allowance isn't necessary; I don't keep house. All the food is here, or delivered by Mr Williams' van and August pays Mrs Stow. He leaves an envelope for her on the kitchen table every Friday. It's sealed so I don't know how much is in it — don't care either. Just want some for me.

It was so lovely at the Windmill going in early on a Friday and having Mr Van Damm coming round to everyone and handing them their wage packets personally. He always did it if he was there. Otherwise his assistant did it. And of course we were paid the extra in advance, if it was our week off. I do miss not having that money. I miss the dancing too, and the music, and the company of the other girls and the laughs we used to have.

Especially about the 'dirty mackintosh brigade'. Those dirty old men (sometimes quite young ones) who used to sit as close to the stage as they could, with their raincoats over their knees.

Fred, our stage manager, used to place stage-hands in the wings to watch out for them. And if they got *too* excited he would inform the house manager who, during a break, would tactfully escort them out of the theatre. How we laughed when he told us!

Now then, I mustn't go on about the Windmill — I mustn't think about it too much or I'll weep . . .

Back to my finances.

The last time I asked Mil to get something for me it was ciggies, and they *do* have Peter Stuyvesant at the village store — I told her I didn't have any money to pay her and hoped she'd say something to August. But of course she didn't. She just said that it was all right because she put everything down on the farm's account. I also asked her to get me a large exercise book, explained that it was to practise my accounts before putting them down in her 'official' account book. And she accepted that quite happily.

Everyone knows her in the village but I couldn't do that in Horsham. I want to have a purse again, and take out coins, and work out my change and how much things cost.

I've plenty of slacks and pullovers and

blouses — nothing smart is needed here, anyway, so quite a few of my things are still packed away and not worn. But I want to look at new cosmetics and magazines, and see what models are putting on their faces and how they are doing their hair. And hats? Perhaps I won't worry about hats — all they wear down here are sensible felt ones, like Auntie.

But I'm beginning to feel like a turnip and long to look into shop windows, and buy a copy of *Vogue*, and I must get some more peroxide. My roots are beginning to show.

Perhaps I should think about giving dancing classes. Perhaps Betty was right; I should be doing something I really love and *then* I could have the money I crave.

But I'd have to get August in a good mood and I'm sure he thinks that now he's given me a bicycle, that is all I need.

Trouble is we don't *know* each other very well — I mean our MINDS — but it is early days and maybe I should concentrate on riding my bike, and going down to the village, and settling in here for a bit longer before I attempt trying to convince my husband that I want to earn my own money again!

I'm sure one of August's favourite expressions would be just like that phrase they used during the war to stop people gossiping. Be like dad, keep mum.

We used to laugh about it at the Windmill and at the thought of all those husbands who didn't like their wives working — but I'm afraid I've gone and married one of them.

Hey ho, I'd better stop this and start on our supper . . .

12

Wednesday

Surprise, surprise, Mil phoned and asked me to go for a coffee this morning! She said should she come and fetch me but I said no, I'd come on Sky.

I am much more confident now and it's only a few miles down to the village and actually I did jolly well and didn't wobble at all once I got going.

I also thought it would be a great chance for me to get away from the farm, see where Mil lived and do some shopping at the chemist whilst I was at it. I'd get my peroxide and other items and put them on the farm's account. Ha!

All of which I did. It is simply wonderful having my own transport and being independent.

Mil's bungalow is on the outskirts of the village (luckily on the opposite side to Betty Folder's so the one won't know when I'm visiting the other). That's the trouble with a small place — everyone knows what is going on and I like keeping some things to myself.

In London one could be completely anonymous and move around with nobody knowing anything about you. It was only at the Windmill, or my end of Barkston Gardens, that I knew other people and was known myself.

Mil possesses a neat little garden in front and a few apple trees at the back, in a sort of orchard. It is very modern and new and she said she bought it when August and I became engaged. She also told me it was a bit of a wrench having to leave the farm but she feels more settled now.

She has a daily who cleans for her, but Mil does all the cooking and has many friends in the village and plays bridge twice a week. She seems very sociable and it's probably far easier for her to pop in and see people there than it was when she lived up here. Though I suppose before the war she was able to drive and get around more. Anyway, she's driving again now but still very careful about mileage, even though petrol is no longer rationed.

I might learn to drive one day. Wouldn't *that* be something!

I quite liked Mil's bungalow although it is a bit poky after the farm. She has a drawing room, hall, compact kitchen and bathroom, a large bedroom for herself and a tiny one at the back for visitors.

She doesn't have any animals but admits she would quite like a cat, so I've offered her a choice of kittens when the next batch comes along. Apparently she never allowed cats into the farmhouse because of August, and Mrs Stow, and the dogs. She laughed when I told her I'd given them all names.

'Ming's my favourite,' I said. 'She's the tabby with the gorgeous green eyes, and Beauty is the pretty little long-haired tabby with the white bib. She's a flirty little so-and-so and fairly simpers whenever Big Black Solomon or Felix is near. I bet she will have the next litter.'

'How do you know them all?' said Mil. 'We just kept them as mousers and they seemed a pretty scruffy lot to me. Although I didn't see them often, I must admit. Do you spend much time in the barn, dear?'

'Of course not,' I said, 'but they are becoming more affectionate because I am giving them a bit of love and attention.' I didn't dare to say I allowed them into the house if Mrs Stow wasn't looking. 'Poor Catty *is* a bit scruffy — she's the very thin tortoiseshell who won't allow anyone near her.'

'But she still has a name,' said Mil, with a smile. I nodded.

'Well, let me know when the next kittens

arrive,' she said, 'and I might as well take one off your hands.'

I think she likes me better now and I learnt quite a bit of gossip from her. Apparently Betty's husband drinks.

I was very surprised. Jim Folder was August's best man but the wedding is such a blur I can scarcely remember him. A small man, I think, certainly smaller than August, but I don't remember anything else about him.

I haven't seen him yet on the farm, but Betty's so sweet and friendly and Jerry's a poppet, I would never have thought there was an unhappy secret lurking in their lives. She has ridden up several times now after lunch. We like to avoid Mrs Stow so we can talk amongst ourselves. But Betty's never mentioned any problems with Jim. She has always come to me up till now but with Sky I'll be able to go down and visit her at home sometimes, then maybe she'll tell me more.

Mil said Jim Folder isn't an alcoholic, or anything dreadful like that, but he goes to The Boar's Head most evenings, leaving Betty at home with Jerry.

I'm so glad August doesn't drink. I couldn't bear to be alone every evening as *well* as during the day. What a selfish and unthinking man Jim must be. I'm not sure if I

want to meet him now. I might say something I shouldn't and, as Mil says, everybody likes Jim and August couldn't manage without him. It's a bit like Dairyman Nick. Why are unpleasant people liked by so many *and* so necessary?

The second intriguing thing I learnt was about that snake-eyed Jean. Jean Tilverton is her full name. She *was* August's girlfriend and they were going steady until he came up to London for that show and met me — ravishing Honey Brown!

Mil says everyone was astonished when they heard he'd taken up with a dancer and discarded that nice young schoolteacher.

Or is that just Mil dropping a tiny bit of poison in my ear?

It would explain why old Snake-Eyes dislikes me. But August can't have been much in love with her if he threw her over just like that. And they weren't actually *engaged*. I did ask him once if he'd had many girlfriends before me and he said, 'No one important'. He admitted he'd been out with a couple of local girls on occasion but was never in love with anyone until I came into his life.

I would feel sorry for Jean if she hadn't shown her dislike so plainly. If she could have accepted me, come across at that 'do' and

had a few words with me like Betty did, I would have really tried to make friends with her. But perhaps that wouldn't have worked. Can a 'has been' ever be bosom pals with a 'here and now'?

Nurse Dickinson has rooms in the village. Her fiancé was killed in a car crash two years ago and she's only a few years older than me but looks much older. Poor girl, no wonder she's a bit abrupt and hard. How can she meet another young man around here? They were very much in love, Mil says, and Lydia Dickinson was a far warmer, softer creature before the tragedy.

She was all right in the car when she gave me a lift home but not exactly chatty. Maybe I should invite her to tea. Though I don't suppose she has much time for that. Perhaps she could pop in on her way to see a patient. I wonder if she and Betty get on. I could ask them together.

Mil also told me that she's going up to London on Saturday. She's meeting an old friend for lunch and they're going to a matinée of *The King's Rhapsody*.

For a moment my heart gave an extra thump as I remembered Henry saying, 'You'd make a splendid understudy for Vanessa Lee, Honey — need singing lessons, of course, but . . . '

How I love that artificial world of bright lights and gaudy costumes and loud music! And how I miss that world I left behind to marry my farmer. The comfort of the buzzing dressing room, the friendship of the other girls, all the excitement and warmth of a show . . .

No, Honey, no.

* * *

I had to get up then and go and make myself a cup of coffee but I'm back now as there's still lots more to put down.

I did wonder a bit how I would feel if Mil ever asked me to go with her.

I could tolerate her on the journey up, and on the journey back, but all day? She does talk a lot. Finding out about folk down here in the village is fun, but continuous small talk for hours on end would be very irritating. But she wouldn't talk right *through* a show, would she? In the interval, I suppose, but there'd be some respite once it all began. Perhaps we could travel up to Victoria together and then go our separate ways? I could go to the Windmill and see the girls again — and meet Henry for lunch.

No, definitely not.

'Give London my love,' I said, before

leaving her, and feeling all goose-pimply and nostalgic inside.

It is not the right time to go back. Not yet. It would be too unsettling and I might not want to return to the farm.

A few more months of clean air and cats, Mrs Stow's cooking, and Betty and Jerry, and Sky are needed. Then I'll go back and be horrified by all the noise and rush and smuts of the city, and be glad to catch the next train back to Sussex.

Perhaps.

Now, now, no more melancholy . . . On my way home I picked some bluebells. I'd seen them through the trees when I went down to the village and couldn't resist them. I thought a great vase of them on the kitchen table would please August when he came in.

Oh dear, that was another mistake. Bluebells don't last as cut flowers. They are gorgeous growing in the woods — they look like a blue lake under the trees — but don't ever pick them. They wilt immediately and collapse in a forlorn sack.

I felt such a fool when Mrs Stow laughed at me as if I should have known, and to make matters worse there was a strange bike propped up against the kitchen wall.

Mrs Stow gave me a queer kind of look when she had stopped laughing and said, 'A visitor for you, duck.'

I dumped the dead bluebells into the compost bucket and went through into the hall in a foul mood. I did not feel like being polite to anyone and thought it might be Mrs Dawson. It wasn't. It was old Snake-Eyes and she was coming down the stairs.

What the hell had she been doing up there?

'I hope you don't mind,' she said, all cool and slithery. 'Only I lent August a book some time ago and wanted it back. No one was here but Mrs Stow knows me and said I could look for it.'

There was nothing in her hands.

'Did you expect to find it under his pillow?' I said, furious that she had been nosing around upstairs in our private world.

She went red.

'I looked on the bookshelves in the dining room and as it wasn't there I thought it might be on a shelf upstairs.'

I sat down, seething.

'If you care to wait, no doubt August will find it for you and invite you to stay to lunch.'

She slid towards the front door.

'Thank you, but I must get back. School lunch is at one.'

'Then you'd better go out through the kitchen. You'll waste another ten minutes trying to get that door open.'

She had to walk past me as I remained seated, and her head was high. I also heard her answering Mrs Stow quite curtly as she went out through the back door.

What right had she to come snooping round *my* house when my back was turned? Book? August never had time to read. Then Mrs Stow appeared in the doorway and she was also red in the face, but it might have been from the oven.

'Sorry about that, duck. I hope I did right but she was so determined when she arrived I didn't feel it was my place to refuse her entry.'

'That's all right, Mrs Stow,' I said. 'You were only doing your duty.'

Then I went upstairs to see if that creature had disturbed anything. It all seemed normal. We always leave the bedroom doors open so she could easily have peered into our room and seen how we sleep — pah!

To cheer myself up this evening, when August went out on his last round, I did my roots.

I do hate peroxide. It makes such a mess of your hands and skin, leaving them all white and wrinkly. But it does the job for my hair and I'm now all blonde and beautiful again. Wish Henry could see me — he would *really* appreciate me.

Never mind, I've got the bottle now so there's enough for several more sessions and I also got some Kotex whilst I was at the chemist. Good old Sky. At least I have some independence . . .

13

Monday

I think I'm preggers! Wouldn't that be the best thing *ever*! I suppose I should go to a doctor and find out but I've lots of time and will wait a bit longer and see. I felt awfully peculiar this morning as soon as I got up and couldn't touch a ciggy until after lunch.

Most odd. I also nearly fainted after my bath. I always have mine in the morning because it wastes a bit of time, but as I stepped out, everything spun round and I collapsed on the bath mat — all shaky and dripping.

I didn't faint but it was a near thing.

I got dressed slowly, wondering and hoping, then went downstairs and sat in the hall — my mind racing. Little July, I kept thinking, little July.

I won't say anything to August just yet, mustn't get too excited, it's *very* early days but oh, how wonderful if it's true!

I told Mrs Stow I had a cold so wouldn't be joining her for a ciggy and coffee in case I gave it to her. She's not much of a cleaner, so this gave her an excuse not to do the hall, or the drawing room, or the stairs, in case she disturbed me.

I did feel foolish sitting there reading and not even *one* ciggy, but I couldn't even face the thought of one and blew my nose several times for Mrs Stow to hear.

I managed a small portion of Mrs Stow's shepherd's pie and peas, followed by a cup of tea, and then felt better.

Thank goodness August wasn't in for lunch so he didn't notice.

I had two ciggies this afternoon so that's an improvement — must see how I am tomorrow.

⋆ ⋆ ⋆

Now for another thing I don't like — it's Wolf.

She is August's favourite and always has place of honour in front of the fireplace, on the rug. Reg, a black and tan mongrel, has to lie in the corner by the grandfather clock. But Wolf is a big black Alsatian with yellow eyes.

She came in this afternoon and lay there in her place when suddenly I looked up from my Agatha Christie (*Death in the Clouds*) and saw Wolf watching me. There was a strange glint in her eyes and I got an awful shock and sat for some minutes, mesmerized by the expression on her black face.

It was so intent I dared not move and thought, God, if that dog attacks me I haven't got a hope.

Mrs Stow is only here in the mornings, and August was out somewhere and wouldn't have heard me if I had screamed. I kept as still as anything and that damned dog kept on looking. Her head was raised, her ears pricked and those eyes never left me.

Finally I made myself look away and pretended to go on reading. I even — VERY CAUTIOUSLY — turned a page. Then after a moment or two, out of the corner of my eye, I saw her lower her head onto her paws and give a short sigh.

It was eerie. Why did she do that? And would she ever spring? I do know her and she knows me, for heaven's sake, and I pulled her away from that hedgehog and shut her and Reg in the shed.

But that was ages ago, I haven't touched her since; she's nearly always out with August. In future I'm going to shut myself in the bedroom, if she's around, and wait until August gets in. I don't want to be on my own with her again. And what about a baby? What if she's jealous of that?

If only August talked more I could discuss it with him . . .

Tuesday

I met Betty's Jim this morning. Although I was prepared to dislike him, he's really very nice. He came up mid-morning and as I was feeling much better today, he stayed and chatted and I found him excellent company. He said he remembered me very well from the wedding and how beautiful I looked. Ha!

I told him it was Mil's wedding gown and as it had fitted me really well she had let me borrow it. I also said I was sorry I didn't remember *him* very well but he agreed that it had been a very busy day and a bit of a rush until we left to catch our train.

Jim is quite small compared to August, with a craggy tanned face, clear blue eyes and light brown hair. I can see Jerry in him when he smiles. His hands are big and look gentle and I should imagine animals feel safe with him.

Mrs Stow made him a cup of tea and I had one, too. I'm not normally a tea drinker, well, not in the morning, but that hot sweet cuppa tasted jolly good. As well as being off ciggies I'm also off coffee. I *must* be pregnant!

Jim Folder has a soft deep voice and made me feel I could confide in him. He wanted to know all about me and how I was enjoying country life, and was I missing my dancing and friends in London?

I don't know if Betty has told him anything but *what* a difference between him and that insolent dairyman, Nick!

I might ask Jim about Wolf's strange behaviour one day, but I'd better speak to August first. He mightn't like me talking about his favourite dog behind his back.

I wish I had a doctor like Jim. Then I'd go and find out about the baby straight away. But the doctor in the village — Dr Wood — is a round, fat, jolly little man who cracks jokes and lets off loud explosions of laughter. I've only met him once, when I was introduced by Mil out in the street. Perhaps knowing that I was a dancer affected him?

I think he wants to be regarded as a good sort, and a chum to everyone — yuk — but he antagonized me and I don't want him touching me with his pudgy pink hands.

Jim's are trustworthy hands — kind and calming — and I should think he'd be good at a birth. Apparently he delivered Jerry. Betty left it too late to get into the hospital in Horsham, so Jim and Nurse Dickinson were with her.

It must be nice to have your baby in all the comfort of your own home, and not amongst starched strangers in a red-brick building.

I wonder if August would let me have little July here? I must ask him when he's in a good mood. He seems very edgy these days and it's even harder to talk to him than usual. That's why I haven't mentioned Wolf yet.

He was awfully cross when he came into the kitchen and found me and Jim nattering away at the table.

'I thought I heard your car ages ago,' he said, as Jim stood up. 'I didn't realize I'd find you sitting here at your leisure. There's work to be done in the barn, man.'

Jim apologized and said he was just introducing himself to me as we hadn't met properly before.

'Keep your gossip for the pub, will you?' said my husband rudely. 'I need you outside.'

He stalked out in a foul temper, making me squirm. But Jim just smiled and gave me a quick pat on the shoulder.

'Don't mind him,' he said. 'He's probably hungry. I'll get down there and see what he wants. Lovely meeting you, Honey, and thanks for the tea, Mrs Stow,' he shouted over his shoulder. 'When August comes back give him some food and he'll soon recover his equilibrium.'

I grinned weakly as he went out. What a nice man. It was hard to believe that he left Betty alone in the evenings and spent his free time down at The Boar's Head. Had Mil been exaggerating?

I'm not too sure about my mother-in-law. Now I'm wondering if she asked me to go and see her on Wednesday in order to get me out of the house, and old Snake-Eyes in?

I don't know either of those women very well but they know each other, and it does seem odd that Jean Tilverton came sniffing round on the very morning I was invited out by August's mother.

⋆ ⋆ ⋆

I do like Jim Folder, though, and can't believe *he* would ever be two-faced. Why can't August be comforting like that? All he ever seems to do these days is criticize when I'm longing for some love and encouragement. And I don't see why it is always *me* who has to seduce *him*. Why can't he ravish me, for a change?

Oh dear, now I'm being grumpy — it must be little July inside me disrupting my thoughts.

And perhaps August will become a

changed man when he learns he is to be a father!

Wednesday

Mil motored up this afternoon in her little black Austin and I was surprisingly glad to see her. I was worrying about Wolf, and about August, and wishing I could smoke and enjoy coffee again, and feeling really out of sorts when she popped in.

I told her I had seen Jim Folder and really liked him.

'But August got awfully annoyed when he found us sitting here over a cuppa and chatting,' I said. 'I can't seem to do anything right these days. Why is he so irritable? Has he always been moody?'

Mil put the kettle on, which I didn't mind at all. Then she sat opposite me at the kitchen table.

'August is probably jealous,' she said. 'Don't look so surprised. Has it not occurred to you that you're a pretty girl and having been on the stage simply adds to your allure? Especially down here. All the men in the neighbourhood are probably dying to get a look at you. It's no wonder August is a bit on edge. He's found himself a treasure and is scared one of his mates will whisk you away when he's not looking.'

I stared at her. She had never said anything so complimentary to me before.

'Thank you for that. I am doing my best to make him a good wife but everything is so new and so different on the farm, I don't think I'll ever be as capable as you.'

She smiled in return. 'I was scared at first that you would miss the bright lights and glamour of the stage and feared that you would find our country living dreadfully dull. And August is not easy, my dear, with his moods and silences, but bear with him.

'You are bright and vivacious and just the person to liven him up a bit. Jim's all right: he and August have known each other since childhood, but next time he comes suggest that he goes to see August first, then they can both come back for a cup of tea afterwards.'

Very wise. I shall do that. Then I told her how surprised I was to know about Jim's drinking. He had seemed such a sympathetic and considerate person to me.

'Jim's a nice boy,' said Mil, 'and the fault isn't all on his side, you know. Much as I like Betty, I can see she is also to blame.'

'Betty is? Why?'

'She is a nagger,' said Mil. 'You will find out in time that she niggles away about things which are quite unimportant. But she does go on. Trouble is, she's really only interested in that pony. Yes, and her son,' she added quickly, seeing my expression. 'But she's no good at housekeeping, Honey, hates cooking and cleaning, and so all her little irritations mount up and she takes it out on Jim when he gets home.'

I supposed Mil had heard all this from August, as he and Jim were old friends, but it did make me wonder what she thought about *me*. After all, my cooking and cleaning and housekeeping skills were as non-existent as Betty's — but I did have Mrs Stow to help me. And I didn't nag my husband. And I didn't much like that talk about the Folders' private life. Perhaps it wasn't August. He didn't seem like a gossip to me.

Mil rattled on.

'Off Jim goes to the pub where there is pleasant male company and nobody cares if his boots are muddy, or if he smells of pig, or if he smokes too much,' she said.

As she got up to go she said:

'Give August a baby, Honey. All men need pride in themselves and in their family, and I should be delighted, as well. I'm longing to be a grandmother.'

'Oh, Mil,' I nearly hugged her, 'there might be one on the way. I didn't want to tell anyone so soon but there — now I've told you.'

She caught hold of my hands and there was genuine warmth glowing out of her.

'Honey, how wonderful! Go and see Dr Wood as soon as you can and get it confirmed. Then you can tell August. This house needs a baby in it — several, I hope. What splendid news, dear.'

She went away all excited and enthusiastic and I felt pretty good, myself. Until I thought of that doctor. I really did *not* want to see him and have him exploring my body with his fat pink hands.

14

Friday

There is no baby.

I missed one period and was late this month so that was why I hoped so much. But I wish I hadn't told Mil. Now I will have to un-tell her.

Betty knows. She came up most unexpectedly this morning and I was on the lav and couldn't leave it for a while. Such a huge amount came pouring out — I'm sure it was the beginning of little July.

I have always had heavy periods and luckily our leader at the Windmill, understood and rearranged routines with other dancers when necessary, as there were several of us with the same problem. We all had stand-ins so the show could go on no matter what time of the month it was.

I really like those new towels which are coming over from America. Thank heavens the chemist here stocks them. They are much lighter than the huge pads we had to wear at the Home. But when I was at Miss Griggs' it was all right because we wore jockstraps, which held up our tights and held us up nice and firm, as well.

Of course, at the Windmill we never wore jockstraps, and didn't dance when we had a period.

Anyway, this morning everything came out and I felt so weak and ghastly I didn't think I'd ever leave the lav.

Then, thank goodness, Betty arrived and when she came upstairs I called out to her and told her where to find some Kotex, and she was wonderful and so calm and soothing I felt better at once.

She left Jerry with Mrs Stow and put me to bed — in the pink bedroom. I didn't have the strength to tell her we slept at the back and I had been caught out in that lav because I'd been searching in the box room for my birth certificate.

Luckily I keep packs of Kotex in that wardrobe. I'd move them if we ever had an overnight guest, which seems highly unlikely, but the little cupboard in our bedroom isn't big enough.

Betty brought me up a lovely sweet cup of tea and gave me some aspirin. She told Mrs Stow I had a dreadful migraine and asked if I wanted her to phone the doctor but I said NO! Mrs Stow is a dreadful gossip and I didn't want the whole village knowing about poor young Mrs Blake, and I hadn't said anything to August.

Mil, I will tell in my own good time.

Betty stayed for lunch and entertained August and told him I was sleeping my migraine off. Bless her.

And I *did* fall asleep but she waited until I woke up and was sure it was safe to leave me alone before riding home again.

Jerry was ever so good in the kitchen. Betty found an old playpen in the box room, must have been August's. And she set that up for Jerry, with a saucepan and wooden spoon — hope Mrs Stow didn't mind the noise — and he was so happy and content there. I do hope our little July — when he or she comes — will be such a darling.

Betty is a good friend — don't know what I would have done without her. I must think of a way to thank her properly. Can those words of Mil's really be true? She has never once said anything nasty about Jim, or moaned at all. But perhaps I don't know her well enough for private problems to come out?

* * *

August was also sweet — the gentlest and most caring he has been since our honeymoon. I explained about having a bad period *and* a headache, and he made supper and I put on my dressing gown and joined him in the kitchen. He made delicious scrambled eggs on toast, and Mrs Stow had left a gorgeous pan of home-made soup, and I ate really well. It was so cosy and comfortable, just him and me.

Then we sat on the big sagging sofa in the hall and listened to some beautiful music on the wireless and I felt very happy. The dogs were with us and Wolf was totally relaxed knowing August was there. I was also content. I had my husband again and everything was right between us — except for losing our baby.

But there will be more, I'm sure of it, and the next will live.

Monday

Mil was very nice about the baby when I saw her this morning, and promised not to say anything to August or Mrs Stow. I know she was dying to ask if heavy periods, or miscarriages, ran in the family, but how could I have answered that? Who knows what I have inherited?

I must find my birth certificate and see what is written on it, I'm sure it must be in one of the cases I brought with me from London. Don't feel like going back into the box room just yet, though. Not that a birth certificate can help much. I mean, can one ever trace back into one's past if one is illegit and brought up in a Home?

I wonder how I got there. Never thought to ask Matron and now it's too late. But the names of my parents and the place I was born should be on it, shouldn't they?

Anyway, August loves me and chose me to be his wife, and I am happy here and have good friends in Henry and Lyn — *must* write to her — and now Betty Folder. That's all I want for the time being.

I suppose, when I have children, they will want to know about their mother's history, so then I'll have to make the effort to discover more about Annie Brown's past.

* * *

I told Mil I won't say I'm pregnant until I begin to show next time, and she said good idea, and would I like to help with the hens?

I was very surprised because I didn't know there was anything I could *do* to help with the hens. She has always made me feel pretty useless up till now, apart from thinking I was 'bright and vivacious' for August. I can't cook, don't sew and can't even hold a baby in my stomach. So what can I do with hens?

I know the field where they roam. It's on the other side of the yard and well away from Dairyman Nick's cottage, thank goodness, or I wouldn't be keen to go there. But I saw it on my very first visit when August showed me round, and I remember admiring the wooden hut which keeps them safe at night.

Mil said Old Stow 'did' the hens now that she is no longer on the farm, but he is getting on in years and spends most of his time in the vegetable garden. It will help him a lot if I take over so I'm going to see him tomorrow.

It's rather a good feeling (for a change) to feel needed.

15

Friday.

Another week gone — how time flies when one is busy! I like chickens. We have a mix of Rhode Island Red and Light Sussex, so Old Stow told me, and they are so fluffy and cuddly I'd love to pick them up, but they won't let me.

My task each morning is to put on my gumboots. I have my own now — got them in the village where there's a very old-fashioned shoe shop which also sells wellington boots. I put them on the farm's account quite happily — after all, I'm doing work for the farm now, aren't I?

I put on my boots then collect a bucket from the scullery and fill it with contents from the chicken pot. This is always bubbling away on the stove and filled with all the odd scraps left over from our meals.

Actually, that's the wrong order. I do the pot *first* and then put on my boots, which are always left in the little porch outside the kitchen door.

If there's not much in the chicken pot, I

add some meal from the side shed where the corn bins are stored, next to the lean-to where I keep Sky.

I give the hens mash every morning in their feeders and then in the afternoon I go with my bucket of grain, and fling the mixed corn about in the field. Old Stow says that's a good combination of feeds.

I always go the back way so I don't have to pass the milking parlour, and when I get to the field I open the two little doors which let the chickens out and onto the gang-ways which lead down to the ground.

They come out shouting and running, and some even fly (rather heavily) they are so thrilled to be free. I fill their troughs with mash, carry the empty bucket to the water trough, give it a good rinse, then fill the various water containers if it hasn't rained during the night.

Then I go round to the back of the hen house and lift up the flaps covering the nesting boxes and collect the warm fresh eggs which are gold and brown, lying in the straw.

I carry them carefully back to the house and wash them in the scullery, where there is a huge square china sink — used mainly for washing boots and veg — and make sure the eggs are free of droppings and bits of feather.

Then I ask Mrs Stow how many she will be

needing and the rest go in another bucket, cushioned with straw and old sheets of *Farmers' Weekly*, layer by layer. They are collected by Mr Williams' van when our groceries are delivered on Tuesday, and sold in his shop.

Actually, it was rather clever of Mil to suggest hens to me.

a) it helps Old Stow, as she said

b) I am learning something about farm life

c) It gets me up in the mornings. Especially now that the weather is improving and it gets lighter earlier.

I have my bath and am sometimes in the kitchen before Mrs Stow arrives.

I must write and tell Lyn and Henry — they'll never believe it!

Mrs Stow makes breakfast for August when he comes in. I have never been a breakfast person and certainly not an 8 a.m. one. I've never been up at 8 in my entire adult life. Except on those Sundays when we had to go to dress rehearsals for the new shows. However, Honey Brown is now Honey Blake and trying to be a good farmer's wife — apart from skinning rabbits — and she'll do her best to accept the many changes in her new life.

August doesn't seem to mind not having porridge made for him at five o'clock, thank goodness, and gets his own cup of tea and a slice of bread, I think, before going out. He did ask if I'd like a cup of tea in bed before he went but I said no, thank you, as kindly as I could.

Can't imagine anything worse. I did have to suffer it bcforc wc married when I came down for those few visits. Mil insisted on bringing a 'nice cup of tea' to the pink bedroom at about 7.30 a.m. but thank goodness those days are over now.

Good old Mrs Stow makes August a generous fry-up and I get out of the kitchen quick. It was especially bad when I was carrying little July — I didn't get up so early then and could *smell* the awful fumes of frying coming up the stairs.

Now I am brighter and happy about the hens, and after my bath I bounce downstairs, say good morning to Mrs Stow, kiss my husband, then leave them both as I go out to do my task.

It's only when I come back in again and before I wash the eggs, that I have my first drink of the day: coffee (I'm back on it now) and a ciggy. Mrs Stow also smokes and joins me at the table with her cup of tea and a Woodbine.

I'll have to write to Henry and ask him to bring several tins of Nescafé with him next time he comes. I have finished mine and hate all the time it takes to make fresh coffee. Mrs Stow is very good and tries to have it ready for me when I come in, but oh, for instant!

* * *

What is really lovely is that the cats have now discovered that I am out and about at an early hour (for me) and they come and join me as I plod across the field.

We make a little convoy with me leading with my bucket and boots, Ming leaping merrily fore and aft, Big Black Solomon and Felix following more sedately and Beauty following the boys. No sign of Catty, of course, but Laurel and Hardy often bring up the rear. They are rather nondescript tabbies and I don't know their sex.

The hens don't seem to mind the cats — I don't think cats attack chickens, do they? Though I'll have to be careful when baby chicks arrive!

The cats wait patiently for me to do the mash and water and collect the eggs, then we all plod back to the house together. If they are lucky they'll get some milk and a few slices of cold meat outside the kitchen door, if Mrs Stow isn't looking.

She won't allow them in the kitchen.

'Thieving beasts,' she calls them. That is one subject we do not agree on (and Dairyman Nick) but her husband is a cat lover and I've made friends with him now.

I think Old Stow was really pleased when I took over the hens and I'm going to help him in the garden come fruit-picking time. He says it'll be good to have assistance with all the currants and gooseberries and raspberries coming at once, and Mrs Stow is going to show me how to bottle.

Bottling fruit! That will be the second Farmer's Wife's Task I will learn. Who knows, JAM may be next!

Old Stow hasn't got any teeth. I could scarcely believe it when I first noticed. Then I asked Mrs Stow, tactfully, how he managed to eat anything with just gums. She said they've hardened up and he can manage most things now. But apparently he has a full set of dentures which are very uncomfortable so he only puts them in on Sundays so he can enjoy the roast.

At first I found it difficult to understand him with his country voice and no teeth. Mrs Stow speaks more clearly. But I'm getting used to Old Stow now, and he's teaching me lots of things.

First it was Sky, then the chickens and now it's Catty.

This morning I had finished the hens and was passing the vegetable garden when I saw Old Stow in his shed, having his mid-morning break.

There was a flask on the ground beside him; he was sitting on a large upturned flower pot and cutting slices off a chunk of cheese with his penknife.

What made me stop and stare was the fact that Catty — CATTY, the untouchable, slink-away-round-the-corner misery — was sitting up very close to his boots and being handed pieces of Old Stow's cheese!

I went up to speak to him but Catty immediately ran off into the hedge.

'How did you do that?' I said, and explained that I had given all the cats names and had managed to make friends with them all except her.

'Dunno,' he said, through his gums. 'Known her a long time, I have. She likes her bits of cheese.'

Amazing. I am going to stroke her one day, I really am.

I'm also going to help Old Stow with the weeding. He says weeding's hard these days as his knees are giving him what for, and I really *need* to use my body more. So when I have an hour or two to spare — from what? Reading, smoking, chickens — I'll pop into the vegetable garden and give him a hand with the hoe.

Unless it's raining. Or perhaps I can find a funny mackintosh hat and raincoat — like Christopher Robin — and wear that when it rains. I've got the waterproof boots now so I'd better go down on Sky and see if I can buy something suitable in the village. Then charge it to the farm's account, of course.

16

Thursday (June already)

I had another lovely day yesterday.

Henry phoned at the beginning of the week to say he'd got my letter and could he come down again with a friend, and that he'd bring five tins of Nescafé with him.

I was thrilled about the Nescafé but wondered about the friend. Was it male? If so, I'd know for certain that Henry was queer.

He refused to give a name when I pestered him, and said he just wanted to warn me that there would be two this time, and could I let splendid Mrs Stow know that they were coming to enjoy her wonderful cooking.

I told him Wednesday would suit as August would be out for the day. I knew my husband wouldn't be keen on meeting Henry *plus* one of his chums. Although having two in the house would prove to August that I was *not* fornicating during his absence and there wouldn't be a row like there was the last time Henry had been.

Luckily Henry decided Wednesday would be fine. Mrs Stow was thrilled to bits, and I thought I would dress up in a slinky top and tight trousers and *heels*, which I hadn't worn since being on the farm — apart from the ones I use to seduce August in the bedroom.

Unfortunately, both the top and trousers were unpleasantly tight so I had to change before they came into a sloppy shirt and my loose slacks — and flat shoes.

Is it because of my lost baby, I wonder? Or have I been putting on weight with all this country living? Bother. I must try and do some exercise every day — but not like Betty's attempts at the barre!

I washed my hair on Tuesday night so that looked all right, and put on my make-up with great care. I don't always wear it these days. The cats and chickens don't notice my face, August doesn't care, and Mrs Stow and Old Stow don't need to be impressed.

But Henry was another matter. And his friend. I had to prove to them that Honey Brown (that was) could still look good — if a bit overweight — and that being a farmer's wife had not changed her.

* * *

He wasn't queer. He wasn't male. He was Lyn!

When I saw the taxi coming up the drive I

raced out to stand in front of the house, smiling and waving.

Thank goodness it wasn't raining so my hair looked good.

Then, on my side of the taxi, the door opened and those fabulous legs appeared.

I shrieked and ran forward and as Lyn straightened we flew into each other's arms.

Poor Henry was quite forgotten.

But he paid the driver and asked him to come and collect at half-past four, which was a good idea, then he came round the back of the taxi as we faced him, grinning, our arms around each other's waists.

I couldn't believe it. And she looked so *smart* — no gumboots for her!

Lyn was wearing high black patent heels and a really full black skirt with a red jacket, neatly waisted, and there were splendid straight seams down the backs of her stockings. *Not* painted on, I checked.

'I've brought some nylons for you, Hon,' she said. 'They're easier to get in Paris.'

A glorious cream silk blouse was under her jacket, which suited her blonde hair, all smoothed up into a sleek chignon. Pearls were around her neck and in her ears and — envy, envy — a gorgeous wide straw hat was on her head.

She was also wearing make-up. I hadn't

seen another female wearing lipstick and powder and mascara since being in Sussex. Apart from Betty Folder, whose lipstick was the wrong colour and usually smudged.

Lyn was carrying a black patent handbag over one arm and a loose black coat over the other. Hardly country clothing! But she looked a dream.

'It's Dior's New Look, Hon,' she said. 'Do you like it?'

'It makes me feel a real country bumpkin,' I said, 'but you look marvellous. Come and see my new home.'

I led her into the kitchen where Mrs Stow almost curtsied, wearing her cherry-pink apron specially found for the occasion. She was all pop-eyed and gaping-mouthed.

I introduced them and Henry greeted Mrs Stow like an old friend as he placed five tins of Nescafé on the table. Was I glad to see those!

I asked how much they were, hoping there would be enough in the pot on the shelf marked LAUNDRY MONEY. I don't want him and Lyn knowing I have no cash of my own but thank goodness Henry said Mrs Stow's fine cooking was payment enough. Bless him. Then I took them through to the drawing room to show off.

I'd arranged roses in two big vases that

morning, and with the sun shining, although not into the room at that hour, everything looked pretty and fresh and it wasn't too cold in there.

The roses are called Albertine and are ramblers, says Mrs Stow, and boy, do they ramble! All over the fence at our end of the vegetable garden and with a fantastic scent. I love them, even if they are pink. Pink flowers are fine; it's just pink garments I don't care for — especially not pale pink twinsets.

We sat down and talked and talked. At least Lyn and I did. Henry just listened and smiled and watched, sitting back in his chair and looking remarkably relaxed.

He was dressed much better this time in a tweed jacket and a mauve tie and dark purple trousers.

'I've just popped over to see Mum and have a short break,' Lyn explained. 'I'm seeing my dentist and a few old friends, and wanted to see you most of all — so here I am.'

'She only arrived yesterday,' said Henry. 'You should feel honoured, Honey.'

Lyn didn't talk about her dancing. She wanted to know all about me, and the farm, and August, and as I hadn't had a visit — or for so long (not since Henry's last) as Mil and Betty are locals and don't count — I jabbered on. After we'd had coffee and biscuits I took them outside.

Lyn put on one of August's old pair of boots with some thick wool socks, which I got from his drawer upstairs. They fitted quite well with her being so tall. But Henry just hovered in his smart town shoes, saying he'd been before and didn't much care for mud.

Actually it wasn't too bad in the yard, and as I led her across, I prayed Dairyman Nick wouldn't be around. The milking parlour was empty but as luck would have it we bumped into him by the calves' pen, so I had to introduce them.

I made it as quick as I could and they were too far away from each other to shake hands, but Lyn looked across at him and I could see how Nick stared at her.

And she did look gorgeous. She'd taken off her hat and her hair was coming down a bit with long blonde wisps across her face, and she was so tall and elegant, even in gumboots, with her full skirt, and black coat slung nonchalantly across her shoulders.

Dairyman Nick's stare was the same as always — rude. I hoped Lyn hadn't noticed as I ushered her away and towards the vegetable garden.

'Wow! That Nick's handsome, isn't he?' she said.

'You think so?'

She glanced across to read my expression.

'Had trouble with him, have you?' She was frowning as she said that.

'Not really.' I shrugged. 'Just don't like him very much. He reminds me of that stage-hand we had at the Windmill. Do you remember him?'

She nodded. 'Insolent,' she said. 'I felt as if that Nick was stripping me naked with his eyes and not paying for the privilege.'

With Old Stow it was completely different. In fact he had been waiting to see Lyn, positioning himself up at the top end of the vegetable garden, and almost hanging over the gate to catch sight of her. So Henry said later.

Because Henry got to him first.

As I led the way through the gate and on past the potting shed, we heard voices down the path and there were Old Stow and Henry deep in conversation. They were discussing radishes.

'I never knew you were interested in gardening, Henry,' I said.

'You don't know much about me, Honey,' he replied. 'I must admit to a wild youth, but as a kid I often helped Dad in his allotment on Sundays.'

Old Stow was beaming at the attention of

such a well dressed and knowledgeable gentleman. And to my surprise he had his teeth in!

He couldn't have known Lyn would be coming, but Mrs Stow must have mentioned two visitors from London to him, and for these special guests, Old Stow had made use of his dentures.

He bowed as I introduced him to Lyn and was unusually tongue-tied. He could cope with Henry, man to man, but talking to such a beautiful woman, who was a dancer in Paris, was beyond him.

Dear Old Stow. What a difference was the admiration in his eyes, and the good honest pleasure on his weather-beaten face, not to mention his shining new teeth, to the cool inspection of Dairyman Nick.

* * *

After an excellent lunch — Henry had asked for exactly what we had had last time and Mrs Stow had obliged — we all washed and dried up as Mrs Stow had gone by then. Then Henry decided he needed a ten minute shut-eye on the sofa, and I took Lyn upstairs.

I showed her the pink bedroom and said that would be hers when she came to stay.

'Don't know when that will be, Hon,' she

said, sitting down on the edge of the pink coverlet and looking at the handbag clutched on her lap. 'Tell you why I'm really here,' she went on. 'I'm having an abortion tomorrow.'

'Oh, Lyn.' I sat down beside her and took one of her cold hands in mine. 'Why?'

She told me she'd been foolish in Paris and had fallen for a chap who was already married but who was a great charmer.

'He knocked my socks off,' she said. 'I'd never felt like that before, Hon, and couldn't cope with my emotions. Silly me.'

She pulled her hand away and stood up to walk over to the window.

'No question of marriage, of course, and no way I can have this baby. He'll pay, which is something, and I'll return when I'm fit and strong. They're keeping my place for me. But Mother doesn't know.'

I longed to tell her about little July but couldn't. How could I say that I had lost the baby I wanted so badly, when she was going to destroy the one she didn't want?

'I'm telling you, Hon, because I've given Mother your phone number. I'm supposed to be staying with you, you see.'

'Where *are* you staying?'

'With Henry.' She came back to the bed and opened her handbag. 'Here's his number. If Mother should contact you and want to speak to me, just make up some excuse that I'm out with August, or something. Then phone me at Henry's and I'll deal with it from there.'

'How long will you be . . . in . . . for?'

'Only a day, if all goes well. Then I'll have to rest a bit and that's where Henry has been so good. It'll only be a few days, Hon, then I'll be back with the girls, I hope.'

She looked so sad I went and put my arms around her and we stood for a while without speaking.

* * *

Now for a happier thought: Henry is going to have one of the next kittens.

Ming and Big Black Solomon and Beauty all came in after lunch when Mrs Stow had gone. And when Lyn and I went downstairs again after our chat, we found Henry stretched out on the sofa with Ming and Beauty tucked in beside him and Big Black Solomon on his stomach. He was rising and falling with Henry's snores like a ship at sea.

That was when Lyn said Henry ought to get a cat. He woke up then, and Ming and Beauty jumped off, but Big Black Solomon took one of their warm places beside him.

'I couldn't possibly have an animal in my

London flat,' said Henry, sitting up and smoothing back his hair and trying to look alert.

'Why not?' said Lyn. 'You've got that fire escape outside your kitchen and those excellent gardens at the back. Have a wooden box made with a proper roof and little entrance — like a small dog kennel — and you can leave it on the steps outside your kitchen window. Then even if it rains, Pussy will be safe and dry until you get in.'

Henry grunted. It was obvious he would like a cat of his own but wanted it to appear *his* idea.

'I'll let you know when the first kittens arrive,' I said, 'and you can make your mind up then.'

That's Mil and Henry taken care of (I know he will agree) and I'll ask Betty if she'd like one. Jerry loves the cats when he comes up to the farm and it would be a way of thanking her for her friendship.

There was a lovely ending to that day.

'Grand finale,' announced Lyn, before it was time for them to leave. 'Remember the dance of the little swans, Honey?'

She slipped out of her jacket and skirt and placed them neatly on the back of an armchair, then held out her left hand to me, still looking fantastic in her black lace undies.

August's thick wool socks were worn as house shoes and I was in my pumps, so we were hopelessly tall and short together — but who cared!

I grabbed hold of her hand with my right, then we crossed our others over our bodies and got our feet into perfect (well, almost perfect) fifth positions on the drawing room floorboards, having first rolled back the two rugs.

'Music, Maestro, please,' said Lyn, and with Henry sitting on the sofa and humming and banging out, 'Rum-tum-tum-tum TUM-tiddly-um-pum, Rum-tum-tum-tum TUM tiddly-um-pum,' Lyn and I danced from Tchaikovsky's brilliant *Swan Lake*, the dance of the four cygnets.

All the older pupils at Miss Griggs' knew that dance but it had been a long time since Lyn and I had tried such a classical number. Our echappé's and pas de chats were definitely wobbly, before we collapsed on the floor, with Henry's loud 'Bravos' and 'Encores' ringing in our ears.

Oh, what a happy day it was — apart from Lyn's sad news. How I wish there could be more of them . . .

17

Friday

Not such a good day.

It was lovely and sunny this morning and as I was feeling restless after Lyn's and Henry's visit, I told Old Stow I'd be back to help him in the garden but just wanted to go down to check on my hedgehog.

It had been ages since I had left him in the ditch but I hoped that I had returned him to the right place and wanted to know if he was all right.

Silly really, because I'm sure one hedgehog looks just like another so I would never know if it was my one, or not. But simply seeing one snuffling about in the ditch, or going about its business on the outskirts of the wood, would have set my mind at rest.

Anyway, I wanted to go and see.

So I left Old Stow (toothless today) grunting amongst the gooseberry bushes with his hoe, and set off, followed by three cats. But as I reached the rise in the field before the long slope down to the trees, the cats stopped. Then Ming turned and raced back towards the farm buildings and the others followed her.

I wondered if she had sensed a fox, but then I smelt wood-smoke and heard distant voices.

It was nowhere near Dairyman Nick's cottage so I didn't worry about him, but I did wonder who was on August's land, and what they were doing there.

They were male voices, talking and laughing, and a dog was barking. I felt uneasy. However, I was Mrs August Blake and this was my land too, and after such a super day on Wednesday I felt brave.

Well, not very. Not brave enough to march purposefully forward through the trees and shout out, 'Hey, you, what do you think you're doing here?'

I crept very carefully forward, hiding behind the trees, and not getting too close. Just wanting to see what was going on so I could tell August about it later.

Unfortunately, the dogs heard me. There were three of them, fierce, scruffy little terriers, and they came snapping and jumping towards me so I had to pick up a fallen branch to fend them off.

'Why, it's the glamorous Mrs Honey,' said the voice I dreaded, and Dairyman Nick came striding towards me through the undergrowth. 'Come and meet my gypsy friends,' he said, with his bold smile. 'They are camping here for a few days.'

That was something I did not want to do. Especially with him by my side. But how could I retreat with dignity? With the pride of being the landowner's wife? I was not prepared; I had been trapped by the man I disliked and longed to get away as quickly as possible. But did not know how.

Instead I shuffled forward a few feet, still carrying my branch, and said 'Hello' in a pathetic voice.

Stupid woman. Stupid weak woman. But I was not expecting an encounter such as this, had not been trained how to confront such a situation as I was in ballet, and with hindsight, of course, it is so much easier to think what I *should* have done.

The gypsy men were very good looking, all five of them, with curly black hair, brown skin and teeth as white and perfect as Dairyman Nick's.

But the females were not so attractive. A very fat grey-haired (greasy) old woman stared out from the open doorway of one wagon, and a baby screamed from inside the other, where a young girl stood — white-faced and rat-like — in a torn pink blouse and long dirty brown skirt.

The two wagons were brightly painted in reds and yellows and blues, and a couple of black and white horses, looking well fed and well cared for, were tethered at one side of the clearing.

Two of the men were sitting on the steps of their wagons; the others stood by the remains of a smouldering fire. They were all staring at me.

Dairyman Nick explained that young Mrs Blake had been a famous dancer in London and had now come to bring glamour and beauty to the Sussex countryside. There was a loud snort from the grumpy old dame at these words, but the men cheered and began clapping their hands. They seemed friendly enough but I did not feel comfortable.

Then, to my horror, one moved forward and bowed in front of me then held out his hands. He wanted to dance with me. Another brought out a mouth organ and began playing some sort of jig.

'I'm sorry, I can't stay,' I said, backing away. 'I've promised Old Stow I'll help him with the weeding.'

I turned and almost bumped into Dairyman Nick, who was standing right behind me. I pushed past and, amidst much laughter and guffaws of derision, I left the jolly group and fairly scurried towards the field.

My face must have been as red as one of their neck scarves but I was *so* glad to get away. I was furious at having been put in such an embarrassing situation and annoyed with myself for not handling it better.

Thankfully, one of the men called the dogs back as I slowed to march up the slope towards the farm buildings.

What an awful encounter.

When I told Old Stow, I was still shaking and couldn't hold the hoe firmly. But eventually I managed to calm down in the safety of the vegetable garden as Old Stow told me August's father had allowed the gypsies to camp in that clearing whenever they passed through the village, and August had carried on the tradition.

They weren't offensive, I thought, and not really frightening. Meeting them like that was just a surprise — shock, I suppose, and if Dairyman Nick had not been there I would probably have been more relaxed about it.

'Their dogs are good little hunters and help with the rabbits,' said Old Stow.

I shrugged. 'I thought they were snappy little things.'

'They're all right so long as the cats keep away. Terrible with cats, they are.'

'What about hedgehogs?' I said, suddenly remembering. 'They wouldn't attack them, would they?' Wolf and Reg had tried and I had carried mine all the way down to that ditch by the wood to keep it *safe*.

'Dogs wouldn't get very far,' he said, 'but a roasted hog is prime meat for them gypos. Pop them into the fire, they do, so they can get all the prickles off, then they roast 'em. Don't fancy it, myself, but Mr Nick told me they tasted fine.'

Well he would, wouldn't he?

I decided not to say anything to August about the gypsies. What would be the point if they were allowed there? But when I mentioned them to Mrs Stow, she said they were not welcome in the village.

'We all make sure our doors and windows are locked when they come visiting,' she said, 'and Mr Williams won't leave his shop for one minute when they're around. Can't think why that nice Mr Nick is so friendly with them.'

As she got our lunch ready she sang —

'My mother said that I never should
Play with the gypsies in the wood
If I did, she would say,
You're a naughty little girl to disobey.
(wagging her finger)
Your hair won't curl, and your teeth won't shine

You're not good-looking and you shan't
be mine.'

As the men all had nice white teeth *and* shiny hair I'm not sure what that song was about but I didn't say any more on the subject, and tried not to think about my hedgehog.

Hopefully tomorrow will be better — but I suppose every day can't be as special and super as Wednesday . . .

18

Monday

No more nasty surprises and I'm beginning to enjoy our Monday routine now. It is always the same.

Mrs Stow does the washing in the kitchen sink, rubba-dubdubbing all the soiled garments like August's shirts and corduroy trousers, and all the cloths she uses. She scrubs away with a great yellow square of Sunlight soap.

I don't give her any of my things. I am quite happy soaking them in the bath with my pack of soap flakes, then either hanging them on one end of the washing line outside or, if the weather is bad, on the wooden horse I've put up in the spare room. I can leave the window open unless it's blowing a gale.

Luckily all the big items like sheets and bath towels are collected by the White Horse Laundry van every Monday afternoon, and returned neatly ironed and folded the following week.

If it rains, Mrs Stow has a clever contraption in the kitchen which she lets down from the ceiling on a sort of pulley: four long wooden rails, on which she hangs her washing and then returns it to dry above our heads.

With all the kitchen smells and frying I don't want any of *my* clothes hanging there, but it's a clever way of drying other things and August doesn't mind. I suppose he is used to it. Thank goodness his checked shirts don't need ironing, or I would have to offer to do them. Good wife, and all that.

Hankies get boiled in a special pot on the stove — not to be confused with the chicken pot!

After feeding my hens and collecting the eggs, whilst Mrs Stow is busy scrubbing at the sink then mangling into a bucket — Lord, what a palaver — I gather together all the dirty sheets and towels and make a big parcel of them on the kitchen table.

Then I wrap them in brown paper, which is kept from last week's clean load, tie them tightly with string so nothing falls out, add a label with our name and address on one side and the list of items on the other, and have it ready for when the White Horse Laundry man calls.

The pot on the shelf in the kitchen has LAUNDRY MONEY written on it in Mil's precise lettering.

From that I take out the amount to pay the driver when he brings last week's load back and collects the new lot. Last time I had to tell him to wait until this Monday as there wasn't enough in the pot and I didn't know where August was. Most embarrassing. But I remembered to tell August to put more money in so today was fine, thank goodness.

Tuesday afternoon

This morning we bottled.

What a tedious and uninspiring job it is, but I'm calling it my third Farmer's Wife's Task. Hens being the first, sorting out laundry the second and now bottling the third.

It was gooseberries today, most of which Old Stow had picked whilst I weeded.

Mrs Stow and I sat at the kitchen table and topped and tailed for what seemed like hours. We nipped off their funny little brown tops and hard green tails with very sharp knives. I wished the girls at the Windmill could see me and wondered — briefly — what they were all doing at that very moment. Then I put all thought of them out of my mind.

Gooseberries need loads of sugar — they are very sour — but because of rationing Mrs

Stow said plain water would do. She said they will be fine with some nice custard on top and we can always add a little sugar when we eat them.

Hmm.

Bottling

First she brought out some very dusty bottling jars from the bottom shelf in the scullery.

These we washed with their rubber rings and their lids.

Then we packed the jars tightly with our topped and tailed washed fruit. We covered the jars with their lids and popped them one by one into the oven.

Mrs Stow said I could go and do something else for about an hour so I went upstairs to the box room and searched for my birth certificate and post office savings book. Couldn't find either.

It is so annoying. Now that I want to find them they are suddenly terribly important, whereas before I just wondered vaguely where they were and didn't really care about finding them.

Back to the kitchen.

Mrs Stow said now that the jars were sterilized we could fill each one with boiling water and put the lids back on.

For future reference —

1. Boil kettle
2. Place lots of *Farmers' Weekly* on the kitchen table
3. One at a time remove jars from oven, place on *Farmers' Weekly*, fill with boiling water. Place rubber ring and lid in position — careful not to burn fingers as they're VERY HOT. Secure immediately with screw-band
4. Re-boil kettle and get next jar out of oven; place on *Farmers' Weekly*, top up with water, etc. etc.
5. When all jars are ready, tighten screw-bands after a few minutes of cooling
6. When cool enough to carry, take into larder and put on one of the lower shelves. Those jars are heavy

There are still black and red currants to do and — Mrs Stow's red face glistens with excitement — later we'll have plums.

Oh, what joy!

Wednesday

I cannot believe it — human contact again after weeks of being an industrious (boring?!) farmer's wife.

Two letters arrived this morning. They are like gold dust. I carried them carefully through to the hall, leaving Mrs Stow fussing away in the kitchen, and curled up on the sagging old couch to read and re-read them.

Thank heavens I had done the hens and we'd had our coffee and ciggies together, so the rest of the morning was mine.

One letter was from Lyn; the other from Auntie.

I wrote to Lyn weeks and weeks ago asking how she was getting on after that horrid event, and now she tells me she is fine. She is back with the Bluebells, completely recovered from her little faux pas, and going out with a much nicer, unmarried, suitable young man.

Marc is a Canadian, she says. He fell in love with Paris after the war and never returned to Montreal. He is a choreographer for the Bluebells, and Lyn says she is very happy.

There was no more news. She's not much of a letter-writer but I was so glad to hear from her and do hope she and Marc will always be together.

Auntie's letter was more interesting. She asked if she could come down and see me on the farm, and if so, which day would suit me and my husband.

So different to Henry who went, 'ring, ring; I'm sitting here at Horsham Station — come and get me,' that first time he visited.

Auntie gave me time to think and to discuss it with August. I wondered if I should ask Mil to tea. The two old biddies might get on well together and it would help with the conversation. Although I'm excited at the thought of seeing Auntie again I'm also a bit afraid — I mean, we live such different lives now. What will we talk about?

Luckily August agreed when he came in. It's hay-making time and he's out most of the day, but he thought it an excellent idea to invite Mil to tea.

So when I've finished this I'll write to Auntie and post it tomorrow. Thursday is the best day next week. I've just phoned Mil and Thursday suits her but I hope *I* will be feeling better by then.

I've got HAY FEVER.

What an affliction to suffer from as a farmer's wife!

When I phoned Mil about Auntie, she asked if I was taking cold drinks and sandwiches to the men in the field?

When I said no, I didn't know I was supposed to, she heard me snuffling and snortling on the end of the line and said, 'Oh, well, perhaps not. You really ought to see Dr Wood, dear, and he'll give you something for it.'

I said, maybe next year, but I know I won't. Maybe I won't get it next year. Maybe this is a one-off?

I intend remaining indoors with my handkerchiefs and hoping it will go away soon. Poor Old Stow has to manage without me but I still do the chickens, VERY QUICKLY, dripping.

I think Mil intends going up to the hayfield herself, and giving the men refreshment. Good for her. She's a far better farmer's wife than I will ever be and *she* doesn't suffer from hay fever.

August has two brothers helping him — they own a small-holding on the other side of the village and August and his mother know them well. They came over that week of our honeymoon, apparently, and also helped when August came up to see the show and met me.

* * *

I'm getting a little bit irritable with this country living, I'm afraid, and must put on a cheerful — if wet — face for Auntie or she will fear the worst.

The drone of the tractor in the distance is a comforting sound but I can't always keep the windows open — it depends on the direction of the wind. And the flies!

Mrs Stow says the small black ones which get stuck on the washing are called thunder bugs, although we haven't had a storm. Wish we could — it might clear the air and my head. But of course August doesn't want rain. He's praying they'll get the hay in before the weather changes.

There are lots of midges about, too. When I go out to the hens they get in my hair and make me scratch and itch in my scalp. I suppose we had hot summers in London but I don't ever remember suffering like this. The air is so hot and dusty. But I travelled to and from the Windmill by Underground and there weren't any midges or hayfields there.

The theatre was hot, of course, but my little room in Barkston Gardens faced north and I always slept well there.

Not like here. August sleeps like a top (where did that expression come from?) but I toss and turn and throw off my covers and long for the cool dawn.

Now, now, mustn't moan — Mrs Stow says I'll be fine once the hay is cut. Just wish I didn't look like this for Auntie — she's sure to think I've been crying and that August and I have had a row.

Evening

One thing has cheered me up — August praised me after supper! I'm sure he was relieved to hear it was Auntie coming and not Henry and he told me he was proud of me!

'You are a splendid wife, Honey, as well as being a beautiful one,' he said, coming to put his arms around me as I stood at the sink. 'I don't think I tell you that often enough.'

'Even with *this* face?' I said, turning round to look up at him through streaming eyes.

'Even with that face,' he said, and kissed me.

'Old Stow says you are helping with the hoeing and Mrs Stow told me you did really well at bottling. Good on you, Hon.'

He went out on his last round and left me glowing. He doesn't often compliment me — he was right there — but when he praises me I feel wonderful. He *does* notice what I'm trying to do even if he doesn't comment very often.

Now I'll write to Auntie — I'm really looking forward to seeing her — hankies at the ready . . .

19

Friday

After I knew Auntie was coming I checked in my smart red Menu Book to see what was entered for Thursdays. Then I told Mrs Stow that it was liver and bacon, mashed potatoes and peas, followed by our bottled gooseberries and custard.

I also asked her to make some of her delicious scones for our tea and, if there was enough sugar, a small iced cake.

It was fun having another visitor from London and I wanted to show off as lady of the manor, even with a blotchy face and red eyes.

Although it was only a few months since I had last seen Auntie at our wedding, she seemed to have aged when I saw her coming through the barrier at Horsham station.

Perhaps it's the dirt of city life which has got into her pores. But I'm used to seeing Mil now and her skin is all soft and pink and pretty, whereas Auntie's appeared sallow and wrinkled. I'm not sure about their ages but I don't think Auntie is that much older than Mil.

Of course *she* wanted to know why I was looking so miserable — had something dreadful happened? So I quickly explained about the wretched hay fever.

Once we were on the bus I forgot about her face, and I hope she did mine, and we chatted away like old friends. We had never chatted like that before but then I was probably too wrapped up in my dancing to talk to her properly. Selfish me. And Auntie was always a quiet sort of person. Always around when I needed her but, even when we lived together, not exactly a 'bosom buddy'.

But yesterday I found her really easy and interested in the farm and, best of all, she had brought my post office savings book with her!

No wonder I couldn't find it here. Mrs Walker had discovered it at the back of a drawer when she was turning out my old room in Barkston Gardens, and as she didn't want to post it she had taken it to Auntie, and asked her to give it to me next time she saw me.

No sign of my birth certificate, unfortunately, but Auntie says she's sure August must have it in a safe place with our marriage certificate.

She also explained that it was a simple matter to change my name. I was known in the village, wasn't I? And I had been into the post office, hadn't I? And everyone in the village knew that I was August's wife, didn't they?

Yes.

Then all I had to do was take my post office savings book down to Mr Frank one day, show him my new signature, and ask him to alter the old name and address. Easy!

Kind Mil collected us from the bus stop and dropped us off at the farm, but didn't come in as she said we would have lots to talk about and *her* time would come at tea-time. Then off she chugged in her little black Austin.

I showed Auntie round the farm at speed because of my eyes and nose — no sign of Dairyman Nick, thank God. And she loved the cats. Now that's another name to add to my list of owners when the kittens appear. Auntie was very surprised that I wasn't affected by their fur as hay fever and an allergy towards cats often go together. Luckily that's not the case with me.

Then she told me about a cat she had once called Nelson, because he only had one eye. But he vanished during one of the air raids and she'd never had the heart to get another.

'I didn't know that,' I said. Of course I hadn't been living with her then but had often gone with her to and from Miss Griggs' various studios, and shopped for shoes etc. But she'd never talked about Nelson.

'I didn't tell you about him, Annie,' she said, 'because I was very fond of him and you wouldn't have understood. But now that I've met Ming and Beauty and seen how much you love them, I think you would understand my feelings. Perhaps I will take courage in both hands and accept a little male or female kit from you.

'You choose it, Annie, and when you tell me it is old enough to leave its mother I will come and collect it.' She smiled; I wished she would smile more often. 'I shall really look forward to having a cat in my home once more.'

With Auntie it will be easier than with Henry, because her rooms are on the ground floor. She will leave the kitchen window open, if she goes out. It's barred anyway but the cat can easily slip through. There are lovely gardens for it to explore at the rear and it's what she did for Nelson, she said. At least we don't have air raids any more, I said, and she smiled again.

Before Mil arrived for tea we had more time to chat. August came in for a very quick lunch, out of politeness, really, then departed, leaving us to wash and put away.

I arranged the trolley ready for tea and

Auntie was very impressed with the little cake and freshly baked scones, and said she hoped Mrs Stow was teaching me to cook. I told her I had already learnt how to bottle fruit and those gooseberries we had for pudding were mine. Auntie was pleased and luckily Mrs Stow had been right and her custard disguised the sourness of the fruit.

We sat down in the drawing room to wait for Mil. Auntie was amazed when I told her that I didn't have my own monthly allowance from August. I said I did ask him once but he wasn't keen on the idea.

'We are struggling a bit financially, Honey,' he had explained to me, 'so I cannot give you a regular amount of money. But please always ask when you need a bob or two.'

It was clear he thought I had enough provided for me on the farm, and that only a few little luxuries might be required on occasion.

'But I need shampoo, and face powder, and new lipstick, and S.T's. and ciggies, and magazines and — I don't know exactly what else,' I said to Auntie, 'but I hate having to put them all on the farm account. It's so *public*. I want my *own* money and to do my own personal shopping.'

'Of course you do,' said Auntie. 'Get your post office savings book sorted out, Annie, so you will be able to draw from that and I will send you postal orders for birthday and Christmas instead of presents. How about that?'

I wanted to hug her but had never done anything like that before and couldn't start now. So I just gave her a HUGE smile.

'I would love that,' I said.

She nodded. 'Now, I know your surname but what first name shall I use?'

'Honey Blake, please,' I said. 'That's who I am now. Annie is all in the past.'

Then Mil's voice called from the kitchen and I stood up and went across to welcome her.

* * *

On our way back to Horsham on the bus, I asked Auntie something I'd been thinking about for ages and now, with newly found intimacy, dared to do it.

We were sitting on the back seat of the double-decker, and the only other passengers upstairs were in the front, so as we rumbled along there was such a noise that nobody else could hear me.

'Are you my mother?' I said.

She looked very surprised. 'Goodness me, no, Annie! Whatever gave you that idea?'

'You seem to have been part of my life for so long, I did wonder and I don't know what's written on my birth certificate.'

'I found you,' she said, looking straight ahead, 'and I registered your birth — as near to the date as I could. So my name will appear on the certificate. But I'm afraid both your mother and father are 'not known'.'

'How did you find me?'

'The girl who lived down in the basement was actually the one who found you on the doorstep as she was going to work,' said Auntie. 'Elsie, her name was. Not there now; she's married and lives in Swindon. But she remembered that I had some connection with the Home in Earls Court and came and banged on my door.'

Fancy dumping a newly born baby on a strange doorstep. My poor mother must have been distraught to do something like that. And what did she tell her family? Even if she had been disowned, or hiding somewhere whilst she was pregnant, *somebody* must have wondered about the baby? Or did she claim it had died at birth?

How I wished I knew the whole story.

I remembered how low I had felt after losing little July, and Lyn's sad face when telling me about *her* baby. I presumed my mother had not been married and, rather than destroy her child, had given birth and then discarded it. How awful she must have felt, and how I wished I knew her and could comfort her. Say — it's all right, everything worked out for the best, your daughter has had some very kind friends and is now married to the best man in the world.

'I am so glad she allowed me to live,' I said to Auntie, 'and that *you* were the one to take charge of me.'

Auntie nodded. 'I was working then so couldn't have taken you on full time, but fortunately Matron and I had been friends for many years, and I knew she was fully equipped to take in waifs and strays.'

'Was I a waif, or a stray?'

'That sounds harsh but you know what I mean, Annie. Little orphans and unknowns.'

'Miss Lamb,' I said, 'and her littlies.'

'Exactly. Of course, I went to the police and they said they would check all the hospitals in the vicinity, but they doubted that they would discover anything about your mother. And the nice young policeman who came to the house could find nothing from the cardboard box and few sheets of newspaper which had covered you.'

'Was that all there was?'

Those pathetic details were almost more distressing than the fact that I had been abandoned. Cardboard and newspaper. What a start in life!

'You were wearing a little cotton nightdress and a woollen cardigan which someone had knitted,' said Auntie, 'and fortunately Elsie found you quickly because it was very cold outside. You were very hungry.' Her face lit up once more with a smile as she turned her head to look at me. 'When Elsie brought you in you were asleep, but you soon woke up and let the whole house know of your arrival!'

'What did you do?'

'I hadn't a clue what to do,' said Auntie cheerfully, 'but phoned for a taxi and gave you sips of boiled water from my finger and got you to the Home as fast as the taxi driver could get us there.'

'Who chose my name?'

'I did when I registered your birth. My mother's name was Anne and you were so little I thought Annie would suit you. To be honest, Brown was the first name which came into my head.'

So that was the beginning of Mrs August Blake. What a long way I had come since then and how fortunate I had been to be rescued by someone like Auntie.

As I waved her away on the train back to Victoria, I decided to invite her again in a few months' time. Auntie was all the 'family' I possessed and now, knowing the facts about her connection with the start of my life, I felt even closer to her.

Mil liked her, too, which was a bonus. She told me she had found Miss Watson a well spoken and intelligent woman.

Miss Watson. Of course I write her proper name on the envelope when we correspond but it's still odd to hear her called that. She'll never be anything other than Auntie to me.

A good day all round — maybe I'll have a go at seducing August tonight. I'm feeling very happy. But maybe not yet — not till the hay is safely in — he is so exhausted these days and the days are extra long. Perhaps I'll wait a bit longer . . .

20

Tuesday

I am becoming very fond of Sarah, the sow.

She didn't have a name at first and August laughed when I told him. But she is so friendly and fat and gorgeous I had to give her a name, and Sarah suits her beautifully.

She knows me now and loves it if I take a carrot or apple for her to crunch, but most of all she likes being scratched.

I have a special strong stick which I leave lying on my side of the sty. Then I lean over the gate and call her and she comes at once. I scratch and scratch her big heavy body and she fairly wheezes with joy, closing her tiny eyes so I can admire her bristly yellow eyelashes. Sometimes, if I am very patient, I can get her to collapse on the floor of the sty in total ecstasy.

This morning, after the hens, I went across to give Sarah a scratch and say good morning. I hadn't been for ages because of my hay fever, but that is at last disappearing and life is becoming normal again.

As I was bending over the sty I had the

uncomfortable feeling that someone was watching me. Turning my head, I saw Dairyman Nick standing at the entrance to the milking parlour, staring.

He wasn't smiling. He wasn't friendly and relaxing. There was no Hello, Honey, how are you this lovely morning?

He simply looked across at me with his insolent eyes, then took out a pack of cigarettes and lit one, still staring silently at me.

I felt foolish, embarrassed, all tense and jittery, with my belly thrust against the sty gate and a stick in my hand.

I think I *might* have been crooning 'Golden Slumbers Kiss Your Eyes'. I do hope I wasn't, but Sarah likes my singing and that lullaby often does the trick. She certainly responds to my voice more than the hens do.

Anyway, I wasn't going to be scared away so I leaned forward and gave Sarah a few more determined scratches, wishing the man would GO.

'Morning, Mrs Honey,' he said at last, his voice echoing over the yard. 'Fond of pork, are you?'

I wasn't going to answer that.

Why does he annoy me every time we meet? Why do I dislike him so much? I don't know. But I do know that I'll make sure I visit the sties during milking-time in future, and not when that awful man is free.

* * *

When Mil motored up later she found me in the vegetable garden with Old Stow.

As I had done the hens and seen Sarah I was now busily hoeing. To cheer myself up, I was also singing 'We'll gather lilacs in the spring again'. I suppose my voice was a bit loud because Mil looked very surprised. But she was quite nice about it.

'You've got a good voice, dear,' she said, staring at me as she stood on the other side of the garden gate. 'That is one of my favourite Ivor Novello songs.'

'Old Stow likes it, too,' I said, 'and singing helps with the weeding.' And forgetting about that irritating dairyman, I thought.

She nodded then came through the gate and down the flagstoned path.

'What I really came about was to ask if you'd like a lift to church on Sunday? I know August is busy — although he always managed to find time to come with me in the old days. We used to go in the truck because of petrol rationing. Not very elegant, but we made the effort.'

I wasn't sure how to answer her.

Over the past weeks and very gradually, as we seldom have time to talk together, slowly August has been opening up to me about his life with Mil before I came. He was not happy.

The trouble was — is — that Mil is a bossy-boots and when her husband died she took over the running of the farm 'for August'. But once August had finished at agricultural college and returned home to farm, his mother found it near impossible to let go.

That was another reason he wanted to get married.

'Of course I fell in love with you,' he said, during one of our few precious conversations, 'but I needed to get Mother out of the house and my wife into it.'

'I'm not much of a farmer's wife,' I said, pressing my face into the hollow where his neck and shoulder met. We were both naked and lying rather cramped, but wonderfully close on his single bed.

'You are great, Honey,' he said, kissing the top of my head. 'You leave me in peace and don't nag or pester. Both of which Mother found impossible to resist.'

'But she is very accomplished,' I said, thinking of the scarlet Menu Book, and the blue Engagements Book, and the Address

Book, in the writing desk. And of her being a dab hand at skinning rabbits. 'I bet she was a good hostess, too.'

August shrugged.

'Mother is a very capable woman and probably didn't have enough to do once I returned. We didn't entertain much during the war years, and her car was in storage so that made her less independent. But I'm afraid she was driving me and Mrs Stow round the bend with her fussing and interference.'

'Poor Mil.' Suddenly I felt sorry for her and the frustration she must have experienced with not nearly enough for her clever brain and industrious hands to do. 'But she's happy in the village now, isn't she? With her friends close by and her bridge evenings.'

'Yes,' he said, 'and so am I and Mrs Stow.' And he hugged me close with a sigh of relief.

* * *

I remembered August's words as I looked at his mother this morning. She did go on, asking why we didn't go to church. She and August used to attend regularly, she said, and it was very important for us to be seen in the Blake pew, and to show interest in village life.

'After all, Padre Dawson married you, dear,

and when your children come along you will want him to christen them, won't you? And when I die I want him to bury me in the churchyard beside the church. So the family should pull together on this one day of the week.'

'Yes,' I said, leaning on my hoe and nodding at her.

I had grown up with Sunday school at the church at the end of our road in Earls Court. We had made an orderly crocodile in our best bibs and tuckers, marching to matins as we got older with Matron in front, looking like the figure-head of a ship, and Kathryn Jane bringing up the rear with the younger ones.

Miss Lamb came on alternate Sundays when Kathryn Jane was left behind with the littlies.

We used to say our prayers every night before getting into bed — even in war time — even in winter when it was *freezing* upstairs — and we always sang one hymn and said one prayer before class with Miss Laycock.

We also said grace before and after every meal at the Home, none of which I do now. Except say my prayers — I do so long for a baby — but *in* bed these days, not down on my knees.

'I really don't think August will be able to

make it every Sunday,' I said, my conscience pricking me just the tiniest bit. 'But I should like to go if you would kindly fetch me.'

She beamed at me and I thought how her arrival in the car would give me the chance to get dolled up for a change. It would be very pleasing to look pretty and smart again but I would have to check on my clothes. I didn't want another disaster like when Henry and Lyn came — there had to be something wearable in the two cases I'd brought with me from London.

I remembered Lyn's amazing Dior outfit with a twinge of envy. What wouldn't I give for something like that!

Then I thought of lunch. In all the excitement of my clothes I'd forgotten we still had to eat.

'What about our roast?' I said to Mil. 'August loves that and Mrs Stow doesn't come on a Sunday.'

'Put it in the oven,' said Mil firmly. 'Give it a good basting, and it'll be just right for when you return. That's what *I* always did.'

I felt a bit dubious. Sunday roast is the one bit of cooking I do well and am proud of. There really isn't anything that can go wrong, Mrs Stow says, and she's been proved right up till now. But I've never left it alone in the oven for so long.

‘I’ll be here at twenty to eleven to collect you,’ Mil went on, ‘and you’ll be back before half past twelve. Or you could come to me for lunch?’ There was hope in her voice. ‘August could meet us at the bungalow. He never seems to have the time to visit me these days.’

I didn’t think he would thank me for agreeing to that. August and his mother would have to sort out their own problems. But at least I could pacify Mil in this way.

‘I’ll tell him,’ I said, lifting my hoe, ‘but you can count on me this Sunday if you will kindly collect me.’

That was this morning.

* * *

After lunch I went up to the stuffy old box room and opened the window. It was very cobwebby and stiff but I got it open eventually and let in the fresh air. Nobody seems to come in there except me.

I hauled out the case I was thinking of and it was quite exciting finding several rather nice things which I had forgotten about. I was so comfortable in my slacks and baggy tops I never wore anything else. Except to that vicarage ‘do’ which was ages ago and in the cold weather, anyway.

Now it was summer and I found a clever

little dress which looked like a suit but was actually all in one piece. It was a dull blue, necessary for utility clothing, but the gold trim made it look smart and it was long-sleeved but not a heavy wool.

I thought it would do for church, which is sure to be cold inside. I remembered buying it for the wedding of Princess Elizabeth and Lieutenant Philip Mountbatten. I had that week off from the Windmill and had spent hours celebrating with the crowds on the Mall.

And what a cold November day that had been.

I sat for a while on a funny little wooden stool in the fusty old box room, remembering.

I had gone with Cynthia, who was in my group. Lyn had to work, and I caught the Piccadilly Line to Green Park and met Cynthia outside at eight o'clock. Horribly early for both of us but there were masses of people about, even at that hour. Everyone was smiling and laughing and it was so lovely to have an occasion to celebrate. We hadn't been so happy since the war ended with Germany two years before.

It wasn't too hard crossing the park but we had great difficulty trying to reach the Mall.

Trouble was we wanted to be as near to

Buckingham Palace as possible but so did everyone else. There were barricades and police everywhere but we found a spot where we could stand with our backs against a tree. Cynthia was terrified of being squashed.

Luckily there were lots of vans in the park selling hot drinks and buns — we were both jolly hungry because we hadn't had breakfast. There were also lots of makeshift toilets, which we didn't like at all, but had to be used before we took up our final position.

I was very glad to be wearing my navy winter coat over my smart little dress. It was COLD.

We didn't see much of the procession out of the palace gates because of all the people in front of us, but as Big Ben boomed out eleven o'clock, a kind person in the front of the crowd shouted out, 'There goes Queen Mary in her Daimler,' and we could see the tops of the Horse Guards because they rode nice and high.

Then, 'There goes the King and Princess Elizabeth — ah! Isn't she lovely? God bless you, dear.'

We all cheered and waved and called out 'God bless you,' although we couldn't see anything. Then we waited and waited for them to return. We knew the service in the Abbey was over when the bells began pealing out. Then, 'Here they come!' shouted a man, and we saw the tops of the Horse Guards again and heard the lovely clattering of hoofs.

After that it was really exciting, because people broke through the barriers and began running towards the palace. Cynthia forgot about being squashed and we ran together, this time getting a place right up near the railings.

We looked up at the balcony, all festooned and gold tasselled, and shouted, 'We want the bride! We want the bride!'

At about half past one, Princess Elizabeth and her new husband came out onto the balcony and waved to the crowd. I could see her quite clearly in her lovely white gown and long veil and sparkling tiara. Philip was bare-headed and very blond. He is a handsome man and looked good in his naval uniform with a great sword hanging at his side (which I really noticed in newspaper photographs next day) but I prefer dark-haired men, myself.

Then all the other members of the Royal Family came out and joined the happy couple. I saw Queen Elizabeth and the King — rather small and thin; he's not been well — and Princess Margaret standing beside her father. We waved and shouted and grinned until we were exhausted but nobody wanted to leave.

It was a super day despite the dreary weather and I do hope they will be as content as I am in my marriage to August Blake Esq.

They have a little son now, called Charles, and I believe she is expecting again. I feel very far away from London where we always knew everything. I don't even read a newspaper down here.

August listens to the nine o'clock news on the wireless every night but I am usually getting ready for bed (and him! and hoping!) at that hour. I think Princess Elizabeth and her husband are living in Malta because of his career in the navy. I must ask Henry or Auntie for more details when I next write. I feel such a country bumpkin these days — wonder if it's worth asking Mil.

* * *

That's enough of memories — now back to the box room and my search for something to wear.

I decided that little navy dress would be fine. I couldn't find my winter coat but don't need it now. I did find the perky little felt hat which went with the dress — not a bit like Auntie's old basin, nor Lyn's gorgeous straw, unfortunately — but it might wow them in church. I also found my navy gloves, and the scarf which is scarlet and yellow and goes well round the neck of that dress.

Shoes were a problem. Only a pair of clod-hoppers — again utility — which were actually very comfortable lace-ups. A bit like the pair I wore to the vicarage 'do' — but wedge heels. But definitely not chic. And I found those splendid long fur boots which I wore to the royal wedding celebrations but could *never* wear down here because of all the mud and slush.

Of course, I do have that pair of black high heels which I use to seduce August, but I couldn't wear them to church. I only wear slippers indoors now — well, old dancing pumps, and the inevitable wellingtons outside.

At the very bottom of the case were some nice short-sleeved cotton blouses, which I pulled out. They'll go well with my slacks. I also found my 'film star' sandals which I remembered buying two summers ago.

I put them on, pulled up my trousers, and had a look at my legs. Then I went through to the pink bedroom where there's a full-length mirror in the door of the wardrobe.

My legs looked good. Almost as good as Lyn's. The sandals wouldn't do for church but I thought I'd pop them into the back bedroom. They'd make a nice change from the black high heels and might get August even more excited when I'm wearing my stockings and suspender belt. Anyway, they're worth a try.

Rita Hayworth bewitches Gregory Peck. Ha!

* * *

Then I decided I had to get August into a really good mood and pester him again about money. I needed a decent pair of shoes for church. I could cycle down to the village to that dreadfully old fashioned shoe shop where I had bought my wellingtons, and see if they had anything acceptable.

Old-Snake Eyes had been wearing a nice pair of navy leather courts with small heels at that 'do'. I wondered where she had bought them.

Then I thought, perhaps I needn't ask August. Perhaps I could charge them to the farm's account. After all, I was going to church at Mil's request (demand) and would be adorning the Blake pew. So why shouldn't the Blake coffers fork out?

My post office savings book had been sorted out with my new name and signature, but there was no way I was going to spend my precious savings on something like this.

Feeling unusually jubilant and determined, I carried everything through to the pink bedroom and put them on the bed. Then I took off my top and trousers and pulled on the little navy dress with the gold trim.

The buttons wouldn't do up.

Either the dress had shrunk — some hope — or I had grown fat — definitely.

Hell and damnation! I am *so* disappointed. I should have known after the trouble I had trying to get dressed up for when Henry came. Now I've got to re-think my wardrobe for Sunday and get into the village quickly. It won't be just new *shoes* I'll be needing . . .

Help!

21

Wednesday

After doing the hens I cycled down to the village this morning. I left Sky outside Dylon and Sons, Ladies' and Gents' Outfitters of Quality, and marched inside feeling very conspicuous. There was nobody else in the shop except for a very smart gentleman in a dark suit and very white shirt and teeth, with greased back hair.

He reminded me of Jeremy Fisher's friend Sir Isaac Newton, only he wasn't wearing a black and gold waistcoat — just black — who was in the Beatrix Potter book I used to read to the young ones sometimes, when Kathryn Jane was busy with the littlies.

This gentleman was standing behind the polished wooden counter. There were loads of glass-fronted compartments behind him, filled with neat piles of gentlemen's underwear and socks, handkerchiefs and scarves, and I don't know what else.

He moved round to greet me as I entered with a little tinkle of the bell.

'Mrs August Blake,' he beamed, his white

teeth glistening. They were not naturally beautiful like Dairyman Nick's; they were definitely false. 'What can I do for you?'

'I would like a dress or a suit,' I said.

Did everyone in the village know me? Did they watch from their windows when I cycled by? Was it Mrs Stow's chat? Or Mil's? It would be even worse when I went to church, then everybody would be looking at me. Golly. I'd better look my best for August's sake, I thought.

Thank heavens we live miles away on the farm and can spend most of our days in gentle obscurity. At least I can. I suppose August is always meeting people at the market, and at the cattle sales, and the like.

'Mrs Batt!' called the smart, false-teethed gentleman, and out from the back came a little grey-haired, grey-clad lady with a tape measure hanging round her neck. 'Kindly escort Mrs Blake upstairs and attend to her requirements,' he said.

'Certainly, sir. If you will follow me, madam.'

Mrs Batt reminded me of another Beatrix Potter character — Mrs Tittlemouse, and although she wasn't wearing a neat white pinafore I could easily see her with a dustpan and brush, sweeping and dusting the floor.

She led me up a steep flight of narrow but

carpeted stairs to the room above, which overlooked the street. There were rows of clothes hanging on the left and right. On one side were all navy, black and grey garments, and on the other were brown and beige and a few of bottle green.

'We are gradually renewing our stock,' said Mrs Batt. 'The war years were hard with such severe shortages.'

I nodded. 'I was hoping for a navy suit — with a full skirt.'

If I was going to dress up I wanted to look feminine again, and have a protruding bosom, and a tiny waist, and swinging skirts above my long nyloned legs. I wanted to be part of Dior's New Look, like Lyn.

'If madam will go into that cubicle and slip off her, er, outer garments, I will come and measure her.'

Mrs Batt pulled aside a curtain and ushered me into the left-hand area, which had a full-length mirror at the far end, and two walls of wooden panelling on either side. The curtain was swooshed to enclose me in complete privacy.

I took off my jacket and top, stepped out of my trousers, and hung them carefully on the hangers and hooks on one wall. Then I swooshed open the curtain and called out, 'Ready!'

Mrs Batt frowned and came scuttling towards me with the tape measure in one hand, and pulled the curtain to behind her.

It was rather warm and claustrophobic with the two of us in such a confined space, and I longed to open the curtain again. There was nobody else upstairs, no one to see my (half) nakedness, but apparently customers at Dylon and Sons, Ladies' and Gents' Outfitters of Quality, had to be given total privacy.

'Excuse me, madam,' said Mrs Batt, standing behind me and encasing my bosom with her tape measure and noting the size.

'Excuse me,' she said again, lowering the tape to surround my stomach and buttocks.

'One moment, please.' She swooshed the curtain open and shut behind her, and went in search of something suitable to cover my form. No numbers were mentioned so I had no idea what size I was, but when she returned there were two items hanging over her arm. They were a jacket and skirt in the lightest of navy wool and fastidiously lined.

Mrs Batt hung them on the other wall hook.

'Call if you need assistance, madam,' she said, before swooshing away once more.

Having been used to dressing and undressing for class at Miss Griggs', and then at the Windmill in front of numerous other females, it wouldn't have worried me at all if Mrs Batt had stayed. My main worry was — would the skirt and jacket fit now that I was fat?

Clever Mrs Batt. She and her tape measure had chosen well. The skirt was full but not baggy full; it swayed when I moved, and did up comfortably round the waist. The jacket was a dream. It was waisted, with three-quarter-length sleeves, and a little round neck with a neat collar and pearl buttons which did up over my breasts.

Then came a furtive little whisper from behind the curtain.

'Come in,' I said.

In came Mrs Batt with a strawberry pink blouse over her arm. My heart sank on seeing it.

'I don't wear pink,' I said.

'If madam would try it on — with the navy — madam might like the effect,' said Mrs Batt.

She was right. Madam *did* like the effect and felt like the bee's knees!

With the hat and gloves and bag I already possessed, I was going to look perfect for church and that scarf with the scarlet and yellow could be discarded. I found I didn't mind *this* shade of pink at all.

'All I need now is a pair of shoes,' I said, turning this way and that and admiring my reflection in the mirror. Oddly enough, in this outfit I didn't look fat at all.

'Take a look next door,' said Mrs Batt. 'I believe they had a new lot in last week.'

'I'll go there now,' I said, beginning to undress.

Immediately, Mrs Batt withdrew her gaze and her presence, and swooshed out of the cubicle.

When I went outside, properly clad, she was waiting to take my purchases away and wrap them.

'Do you have a flower for your hat?' she asked, as she folded and carefully slid my suit into a brown paper carrier. 'Only I have some lovely artificial blooms newly arrived which I think will match your blouse.'

* * *

I rode home with a very large bag in the basket on my handlebars containing —

a) one navy suit
b) one strawberry pink blouse
c) one very pretty pink and white flower
d) a pair of navy leather shoes with pointed toes and heels which are not too high but look smart.

All had been entered on the farm's account.

How am I going to tell August?

Everything was extremely expensive and I wobbled on my bike thinking of what he would say. Of course I'll have to tell him — but when?

Perhaps I'll ask Mil's advice. After all, it was her idea. I would never have insisted on going to church on my own and August has never suggested it.

Unfortunately, the farm is going to have to pay out a great deal more than a mere bob or two, for my lavish purchases . . .

22

Monday

Mil came and collected me yesterday at exactly twenty minutes to eleven, wearing a sensible suit, pepper-and-salty, with a straight 'square' skirt and a square jacket with square shoulders It looked very war-time to me and probably was. I don't think she has ever spent much money on clothes.

Oh dear, when am I going to tell August about my spending?

Not yet.

Mil was also wearing a sensible peaked hat and carried a brown leather handbag (definitely pre-war) which was big and cumbersome and I can't imagine what she had in it. She held her prayer book in her other hand and had sensible brogues on her feet. Very like Auntie's.

She didn't say anything about my outfit — August had gone out before I got all dressed up, thank goodness, so didn't see me. But Mil did *look*.

I was very conscious of more looks as I followed her down the aisle to the very front of the church (it reminded me of my wedding, only then I had been *really* dressed up in my glorious silk gown). Mil stood back for me to go in first — on the right, second pew from the front. The Blake's family pew.

I was glad to kneel and look virtuous as the organ pealed out and Mil whispered across the aisle to Mrs Dawson. I stayed on my knees (quite painful actually, as I hadn't done it for so long) until the congregation rose to its feet for the first hymn and Padre Dawson's welcoming voice rang out.

Mine must have joined his quite loudly because I saw him glance across at me and give a nod. It was one of my favourites, 'Praise to the Holiest in the Height'. I must try it on Old Stow. And on Sarah, if that revolting dairyman is elsewhere. It will make a change from my other songs and I do love it.

Padre Dawson preached a good sermon — not too long — and he certainly possesses a good singing voice. There weren't many in the choir so his booming tones helped enormously.

At the end we all filtered out and he gave me a very good handshake — nice and firm — and his eyes were kind and friendly, just like I remembered.

Perhaps I will go more often.

'Good of you to come, my dear,' he said, 'and may I say how very nice you look.'

Then he asked if I would consider joining the choir. He *had* heard my singing and he believed I would make a good addition to the choir stall!

I wasn't sure how to answer so said I'd let him know. Part of me would love the dressing up and the theatrical entrance and the glorious singing (and I would look smashing in those robes if I did my face up and made sure my hair was all right) but, oh dear, what company.

There are only two females (as far as I know, unless some were away) both elderly and rather quivery trebles — no wonder he wants me! And the three men standing behind were also elderly and inclined to bellow.

The thought of choir practice — once, twice, a week? — is also daunting. I bet it's in the evenings, too, which is when I like to wait for my husband and spend time with him.

I think I'll have to say no — tactfully.

Then Mrs Dawson swooped, wearing a similar outfit to Mil's — all squares and pepper-and-salt — and invited us round to the church hall for tea and biscuits.

Thankfully, Mil said she had to get me back to August.

'Another time then,' said Mrs Dawson, her pale eyes running all over my new suit and pretty hat with the flower, and my NYLON stockings; She obviously found the entire outfit just a teeny bit showgirl-ish.

Snake-Eyes came up and spoke very sweetly to Mil before turning to me and saying she loved my hat.

Good for her. It sounded genuine enough so maybe we *can* be friends.

I saw Mrs Batt in the background, more Mrs Tittlemouseish than ever and still in grey, but she looked very sheepish and avoided my wave. I was going to go up and thank her for helping me with my ensemble, but perhaps one should not fraternize with tradespeople even in church.

No sign of the Stows but I know he doesn't have time for 'them churchy places' and I think she is Baptist.

Dear Betty emerged from the throng and came and gave me a hug.

'You look stunning, Honey! Please come down and see me one day next week and give me some idea what to *wear*. We can go through my wardrobe and you can tell me what's right and what's not. I haven't a clue.'

She was wearing a beige top and skirt and *black* shoes, and a beige hat (like Auntie's). She looked like a sack of potatoes. No waist at all and very flat-chested. She's so much better in jodhpurs and shirts, which is what she usually wears.

I said I'd go on Wednesday morning and that suits her. She told me Jim was looking after Jerry that morning but she had to rush back as he had to visit a sick cow before lunch.

* * *

On the way home I found the courage to ask Mil's advice about August. I didn't say how much my outfit had cost, but admitted it was rather expensive.

'Learn to cook, dear,' she said, sitting very upright behind the steering wheel. 'You know the way to a man's heart is through his stomach, and August does love his food.

'Learn all you can from Mrs Stow. She's not much of a cleaner but she can cook. Then surprise August with one of his favourite desserts. He'll be delighted with your expertise so tell him then, dear.'

Tuesday

More excitement. We have kittens at last!

When I went to see Old Stow this morning

after doing the hens, he said there was a surprise for me behind the potting shed.

'Go and look,' he said, 'but go gently — don't want to faze her.'

He pointed to the side of the shed where a narrow passage leads between the shed and the hedge. When I tiptoed round I saw a sort of cave under the shed with a bit of sacking sticking out, and when I bent down to look there were five kittens all curled up beside their mother.

Not Ming.

Not Beauty.

But Catty!

Ugly, unfriendly, scrawny old Catty. As two of the kittens are black I reckon Big Black Solomon is the father and Catty has beaten Beauty to it.

Of course, I haven't seen them properly yet and don't dare go too close — but in a week, or so, I hope Catty will trust me enough to admire her babies and then I must decide which one is for Mil, and for Henry, and for Auntie, and tomorrow I'll ask Betty if she would like one for Jerry. The fifth can stay here with his mum and I'll have fun deciding on a name. Yipee!

* * *

When August came in I had to tell him about the kittens, but he wasn't really interested, not being a 'cat' person like Henry, or Old Stow.

So, to change the subject, I decided to mention my bugbear. Get it over with before I had to confess to my extravagant shopping.

'Your dairyman doesn't like me,' I said. 'Do you know why?'

August frowned, his eyebrows drawing together above his nose.

'Nick? What are you on about? 'Course he likes you, Honey. You're my wife and settling in really well on the farm.'

I shook my head.

'He doesn't. Perhaps he resents me taking Mil's place. Did they get on well together? Mrs Stow thinks he's wonderful and he obviously likes *her*.'

August grinned.

'Mrs Stow is an old flirt and likes all good-looking young men. Don't know about Mother. You'd better ask her.'

Then he told me something I didn't know.

'Has Mrs Stow mentioned her son to you?'

I stared at him. 'No, she hasn't. I didn't know the Stows had any children.'

'Only the one,' said August. 'Nice lad. He used to help a bit in the holidays. He was fixing some guttering on their house two or three autumns ago and fell off the ladder. Broke his neck.'

'Oh no!' I covered my mouth with my hand. 'Oh, that's awful. Poor Mr and Mrs Stow, I'm glad you told me — I might have said something about children to her.'

'She can probably talk about it now,' said August, 'but she's never forgiven Old Stow. He should have been holding the ladder but went off to chat to the neighbour when it happened.'

When August went out for his final round I felt really sad. Maybe that was the reason Old Stow was always so morose, and why Mrs Stow was fond of Dairyman Nick — because he reminded her of her son.

I'm going to be especially nice to the Stows tomorrow now that I have been told about that tragedy in their lives, and I'm also going to be nice to Nick.

We live so close it'll be pleasant being neighbourly and I'm going to make the effort, even if he won't . . .

23

Wednesday

I cycled down to Betty this morning and told her about the kittens. We decided next time she comes up we'll let Jerry choose.

'That way he'll feel it's really *his*,' said Betty, 'and I hope it will teach him to be more gentle. Don't let it come too young, Honey. He's a bit rough with his hands at present.'

Jerry was beaming from inside his playpen. Very proud of himself and VERY noisy — banging.

Poor kitten. A boisterous puppy would probably be better. But if Betty keeps Jerry in his pen, the kitten will be able to get in and out through the bars when it needs to.

'They are tiny at the moment,' I said, 'and haven't opened their eyes yet. So don't come for a week, or so.'

Then I asked her why she didn't sing in the choir, and she roared with laughter and said she couldn't sing a note in tune.

That's a pity, because I might have considered going if Betty had come with me.

It would have been fun with someone young beside me.

We went upstairs after she had put Jerry outside in his pram for his morning nap, and, faced with her wardrobe, I didn't know what to say. Such awful baggy skirts and ditto jumpers, all dreary browns and navies and one bright *custard* yellow!

'I knitted that from some wool Mum had over,' said Betty, as we both gazed at the revolting yellow, 'but I've always hated that colour.'

'A bit like me and pink,' I said. 'Now, what do you want clothes *for*, Betty? Is it for Sundays, or every day? You look best in jodhpurs and cotton tops, you know. They really suit you.'

'I know,' she said miserably, 'but Jim says he's sick of seeing me in them and why don't I dress up and look feminine? And I don't know *how* to, Honey.'

'Have you any money?' I said. 'Can we go shopping at Dylon and Sons?' I felt sure Mrs Batt would be great at sorting out her new attire.

'Ooh, no,' said Betty, her eyes enormous. 'Jim wouldn't like that — far too pricey — and he'll say I've got enough as it is.' We both stared again into her crammed wardrobe.

'Right,' I said, my heart sinking at the thought of what August was going to say about my purchases, 'let's get everything out and on the bed and then we can have a proper look at them.'

* * *

As I cycled home I felt better. It had been a good morning with time well spent.

a) Betty and Jerry are coming up a week on Thursday to choose a kitten. Their eyes must be open by then, mustn't they?
b) I had a load of old cardies and jumpers in the basket on my handlebars, which I am going to unravel and make into balls of wool for Betty, just like I did at the Home. I might even knit a scarf for Jerry. It would be better than those disgusting rabbit-skin mittens which he hasn't worn. But then it's summer now and Betty says she's put them away for winter.
c) We sorted out two reasonable outfits for either church, or an occasion: a navy skirt and top with a pretty turquoise and pink Jacqmar scarf which I found screwed up at the back of a drawer.

Her mother-in-law gave it to her when she was engaged to Jim but she's never worn it because she doesn't like her mother-in-law. I

persuaded her that it looked fine around her neck with the navy top, and those printed silk scarves are like *gold* dust these days. I wish Mil had given me something like that and not that pink knitted one.

We also found a pair of flat (but never mind) beige shoes, which are smarter than those awful black things, and I'm going to give her two pairs of the nylon stockings that Lyn brought me from Paris.

Lyn kindly gave me five pairs and as I so seldom wear them, two pairs can easily go to Betty. But I did warn her to beware of kittens and Jerry. I don't want them laddered before she's even left the house.

d) The other outfit was the beige skirt she had worn to church — not lovely and swirly and girly like mine — but all scrunched up around the waist and very full, making her look like a balloon. But when she put it on with a different, darker brown top, and wore her beige shoes and a green scarf (not Jacqmar) around her neck, she didn't look too bad.

Betty's never known what to do with scarves, she said, except wear them on her head. But loosely folded around her neck, they make her outfit look quite chic and I hope Jim will be pleased.

I'm so glad I was able to help her, and she

was thrilled about the nylons and about the kitten.

⋆ ⋆ ⋆

When I went up this afternoon to feed the hens, I had a quick look at Catty. I can't keep away!

I take her little bits of meat we have left over — in the afternoons so Mrs Stow doesn't know — and I'm also leaving a saucer, well, a bowl really — because it's easier to carry and doesn't spill — of milk, which I put outside her little cave and it's always empty next day.

How can she get away to hunt when she's caring for her brood? Anyway, it must help when she's giving out so much milk, herself. I suppose a hedgehog might be taking it, though I doubt whether a Mrs Tiggywinkle would dare to venture so close to a mother cat when she has her kittens to defend.

Old Stow says as long as we keep the gate shut — so the dogs don't get in — she'll be quite safe.

I go *very* carefully because Old Stow is her friend, not me. I crouch there as low and quiet as I can, never put out a hand to try and touch her or the kittens, and talk to her so she gets used to my voice. She's beginning to trust me. This afternoon for the very first time I heard her purring!

I danced all the way to the hens singing 'We're gonna hang out the washing on the Siegfried Line, Have you any dirty washing, Mother, dear?' as loudly as I could. I do love the songs our troops used to sing. We did a splendid programme at the Windmill which went down really well.

The wardrobe department worked like slaves making us smart military outfits: proper khaki jackets with gold buttons and braid, peaked hats (a bit like Mil's Sunday one only in khakhi) and very neat khaki shorts.

We did a jaunty tap number to 'Siegfried Line' ending with high kicks. And the final number was appreciated even more.

It was to 'Wish me luck as you wave me goodbye'.

We moved in two rows, Lyn with the taller girls and me with the shorter ones, and we held up Union Jacks to hide our nakedness, very much in the way I use my bath towel to seduce August. But after we had finished our routine we all lined up to leave the stage and each girl dropped her flag just as she reached the wings.

I don't know if the Lord Chamberlain ever objected; we were never stopped from performing it, and that programme lasted well over the usual six weeks due to popular demand!

After all, the only parts of us that showed in motion were our backs, although naughty Jenny, last one off in our lot, did turn at the end and hold her flag high *facing* the audience before the lights went off. There was *such* a roar of approval!

* * *

Oh, memories — memories. Stop it, Honey, and think about the kittens and plan for the future. You are a farmer's wife now.

I sang even louder as I marched away from the fields trying to forget the Windmill and all those happy days there and I made myself think of Catty, and how I was gradually gaining her trust. And when I took her some milk later today I actually *smiled* at Dairyman Nick!

He was crossing the yard as I carried my bowl of milk through the gate into the vegetable garden, and I raised my free hand and waved at him.

I can't remember if he smiled back — can't remember if he said anything. My heart was thudding so much with the effort but I DID IT! I know it was the right thing to do and from now on surely our meetings will be easier.

The kittens make me happy. The chickens and Sarah make me happy. I love gardening with Old Stow and my friendship with Betty Folder and Jerry. So I'm going to be nice to Dairyman Nick every single time I see him from now on — there!

24

Nothing written for days and days — don't know what day it is — don't care. Don't even want to write now I am so filled with HATE and FURY and DESPERATION.

But I'm going to put down what happened so I have a record of it and perhaps writing will help. Don't believe it will — want to cry, buckets and buckets of tears, and spit POISON. I am so filled with ANGER.

I'm sleeping in the pink bedroom now — can't bear my husband anywhere near me.

Monday evening

Jim Folder saved me — he came up and knocked on the door this morning.

'Honey, may I come in? It's Jim.'

'GO AWAY!'

The door wasn't locked so he came in and stood looking across at me.

'You are a strong girl, Honey, and you disappoint me,' he said. 'I had expected more of you.'

'GO AWAY!'

'August asked me to come and I need your help.'

That surprised me into listening. I lifted my head and stared back.

'I need to catch all the cats,' he said. 'I've brought some cages with me but they know you better than they know me, so I want you to come.'

'What are you going to do with them?' I trusted Jim more than I did my husband.

'I'm going to neuter them,' he said, 'so we won't have this trouble again.'

Slowly I climbed off the bed and walked towards him.

'Where's that man?' I said.

'Gone down to his cottage,' said Jim. 'Don't worry, he won't be about. Just help me catch the animals, Honey, and I'll take them down to the surgery.'

* * *

It was Thursday morning that I discovered they had gone.

I'll never forget that day — never.

I went as usual to let the hens out and feed them, then came back via Old Stow and the shed.

But Old Stow wasn't there. I know *now* that he couldn't face me so had gone round to the back of the barn for a smoke.

Anyway, I was a bit surprised not to see him anywhere about but went humming happily round by the side of the hedge and the shed, crouched low as usual and saw — nothing. Not even the bit of sacking which made their bed.

I couldn't believe my eyes and knelt, placing the side of my face against the ground, screwing up my eyes, wishing I had a torch, thinking Catty must have taken them right to the back for safety.

I called softly — I waited — I called again. No movement — no sound. ABSOLUTELY NOTHING.

I remember thinking perhaps she was scared in the night. Perhaps a fox came sniffing? Perhaps she's taken them away to another hideaway? Blast! Now I would have to search again. But Old Stow should know.

I went round the shed and ran up to the gate. Still no sign of him.

'Old Stow?' I called. Where was the man? 'Old Stow?' I fairly yelled, getting angrier by the second. What was he doing?

Slowly, across the yard, came the old gardener, dragging on his fag, his face more crumpled, and grumpier than ever.

'It's no good hollerin' at me,' he said. 'That won't bring 'em back.'

He shoved past me through the gate and stumped up to the shed where he lifted out his spade.

'Where are they?' I said. 'Where are Catty and the kittens?'

'Gone,' he said, and walked away down the path.

'Gone where?' I ran after him. 'Was she frightened? Has she found a better place? Do you know where they are?'

He stopped, threw down his stub and ground it onto the path with his boot.

'They've been drowned,' he said. 'Dairyman Nick drowned them and Catty's disappeared.'

Then he lifted his spade and marched off to the farthest end of the garden.

For a moment I was so angry I thought I'd be sick. How *dare* that man kill my kittens? And Catty — so full of milk and love — what would she do? Or had he killed her, too?

I was so furious, I wanted to find Nick and scratch his handsome, face until it bled.

He was *not* the owner here. He was a foul, lowly COWMAN and my husband owned this farm and those were MY cats!

I ran out into the yard. I would go to that cottage and tell that so-good-with-the-cows blond beast exactly what I thought of him. Scum!

'Honey!' August almost bumped into me. 'What on earth has happened? Are you all right?'

He put his hands on my shoulders and looked down with real concern on his face. 'What is it?'

I let rip then — swearing as we had sworn at the Windmill when something went wrong during a rehearsal; when we were fed up with particularly offensive remarks coming from the audience; or when we were tired and our legs were aching and we needed a break.

'All right, all right, hush your mouth!' His hand stopped me. 'Just tell me, what is upsetting you?'

'That bloody cowman! That foul sodding brute! That grinning white-toothed ape! He's killed my kittens and he had no *right* to kill them. I don't know where Catty is — she was just getting to like me and I love her and I love those kittens and I promised Betty and Auntie and Henry — '

Then I broke into a torrent of weeping and August pulled me close to his chest.

'There, there,' he said, rubbing my back. 'You shouldn't have got so fond of them, Honey.'

That stopped me. I stepped back from him, scarcely believing what I heard.

'You aren't going to say *anything* to him?

You think it's *right* what he's done?'

'Honey, we can't keep having cats on this place — we have enough as it is, and we — '

'They were MINE!' I shouted. 'I *told* you about them. And I had found homes for all of them so they wouldn't have remained here. Don't you *listen* to what I tell you?'

'I'm sorry,' he said. 'It was a misunderstanding. I never told Nick you wanted to keep them, Hon.'

'So you take his side? It's fine for him to kill what he will. Rabbits, yes. Hedgehogs, yes. Kittens — fine by you. All quite in order on your farm, August, and your wife's wishes be damned.'

'Honey,' he said, trying to get hold of me again but I shoved him off and went back to the house. Seething.

* * *

My head was aching and my heart was aching as I stormed past Mrs Stow and thundered up the stairs.

I couldn't believe that my husband was taking the cowman's side against his wife's so I moved into the pink bedroom. I couldn't bear any more of August for the time being.

I didn't go downstairs again. Didn't care about Mrs Stow or Mil. I don't know what

August would tell them if they asked. I didn't do the hens and needed time to be alone and grieve. To think about what to do next.

And that cowman *knew* they were my kittens. He had seen me taking them a bowl of milk.

Somebody put trays of food outside the door, which I ignored. August brought me up cups of coffee whenever he was in, which I did drink — had to take some sustenance — and I had my ciggies, at least enough for the next few days. But I still hated August, and his cowman, and everybody else . . .

I was determined to punish that man but couldn't think how — wanted to make him suffer as much as he had made me and Catty suffer.

* * *

Yesterday I ate a bit — must have been Mil because it was a roast and Mrs Stow doesn't come in Sundays — but nobody came and knocked. It was just put outside the door and as soon as footsteps departed down the stairs I opened the door and grabbed it. I was getting jolly hungry and beginning to feel a bit foolish but wasn't sure how to descend with dignity. Thank goodness Jim Folder came up this morning and gave me a chance to re-appear with pride intact . . .

* * *

We managed to get hold of Big Black Solomon — always a relaxed and friendly cat — and Felix and Beauty followed him.

Ming was less agreeable. But she likes me and she likes the titbits I sometimes give her from the larder. So with a lot of fuss and coaxing, I eventually lifted her up and gave her a cuddle before thrusting her into one of the containers in Jim's car.

The other two — Laurel and Hardy — had to be tempted with more titbits but we got them in, too. So it was only dear bereft Catty whom we were unable to find and Old Stow was no help at all.

He was even grumpier than ever and would hardly speak to us. I think he's annoyed because I haven't been doing the hens, haven't been weeding for him, haven't been *seen* for days. And I'm sure he's missing Catty, although he'd never admit that.

In the car I had an idea. I asked Jim if I could have one of his cages when we had finished with them. When he wanted to know why, I said I would leave it in the potting shed for Old Stow. He knew Catty, and she knew him, and she *might* come back one day. Then Old Stow could pop her in the cage, let me know, and I'd phone Jim and tell him.

Jim agreed so on we went with our precious load. There was no sign of August, or that wretched cowman, and Mrs Stow is viewing me from a distance. I think I mean she is keeping a respectful distance from me? Whatever . . .

I wanted to see my cats safely settled and Jim didn't mind me going with him. I said I'd walk back — didn't care about the three-mile trek and knew the exercise would do me good and burn up some of my fury.

But Jim said I couldn't possibly carry a cage all that way and as he had a farm to visit on the Horsham Road, he'd drop me off at the bottom of our track.

His office and surgery are in the high street, beyond Dylon and Sons, past the chemist and the library, almost at the end of the village.

Gladys is his receptionist and nurse, and she sits behind the counter in a crisp white uniform, looking very welcoming. She wasn't at that vicarage 'do' — don't suppose she could spare the time — so I only met her once before when Mil was showing me round the village.

Gladys takes telephone messages, writes

Jim's letters, and does his accounts and the filing. She also looks after his patients at the back. There are never very many of those as Jim is mainly an outdoor man. In fact, my cats were the most he had ever had at one time.

I told him to put the bill on the farm's account but he just looked at me.

'We'll see,' he said.

He is such a good friend of August's, I'm glad that he's accepted me. I suppose seeing so much of Betty and little Jerry, also helps. But I'm not going to think about them — won't think about my kittens. And then there's Auntie and Henry I'll have to tell. But not yet.

I'm not going to think about anything except making my cats safe and no more dead babies. Although I don't suppose they'll thank me for what I'm doing to them. Can neutered cats still mate? I don't suppose they can because eunuchs don't, and that's why they're safe to guard the ladies in a harem. Well, at least there won't be any more slaughtered kittens, Mr Cowman.

Behind Jim's office are two rooms — one for surgery with an operating table, and the other filled with numerous cages and containers where sick animals stay.

He only has surgery here on one afternoon

a week, as most of the time he is travelling around local farms. But I knew my cats would be safe and cared for by Gladys, and wouldn't be confined for too long. They are going to hate being shut up but it is for the best. If only I could tell them that.

'I'll bring the males back in a day, or two,' Jim said, in the car. 'But the females will have to stay longer until their stitches have been removed.'

I nodded. I would have agreed to anything Jim Folder said. I trusted him completely.

'Do *you* like Dairyman Nick?' I asked suddenly, wondering why I was the only person to dislike him. Perhaps there was something wrong with *me*. But I didn't think so because I'd always been able to make friends in my dancing world, and Mil now welcomed me, and Betty, and the Stows. But even *before* the kitten disaster I had disliked Dairyman Nick and felt he disliked me. Why?

Jim was silent for so long that I knew he didn't like the man but wasn't going to admit it. Then he glanced sideways at me.

'Why do you ask, Honey?'

'He hasn't tried anything on,' I said quickly, 'he wouldn't dare, or I'd knee him where it really hurts! But he has never liked me, nor me him — and *don't* tell me he's a good man with cows!'

'I won't.' Jim shook his head. 'And in a way you should be grateful to him, Honey. It was Nick who chose you.'

'CHOSE ME!' I screeched.

Jim tutted. 'Sorry — bad use of words — forgive me. Only he and I were amongst the group of August's friends who went up for that night out in London. I don't suppose you remember us — you and August were so wrapped up in each other — but we were in that little restaurant after the show, thinking that August had done all right for himself meeting you.'

I banged my fists down on my knees. 'Stop the car — *now*, Jim Folder. And tell me exactly what you mean.'

My heart was pounding and I dreaded what I was about to hear. How had that man *chosen* me?

Jim tutted again before pulling the car to a halt at the side of the lane. Then he braked hard and switched off the engine. Behind us one of the cats was mewing piteously, but we ignored it.

'Lord, August will kill me for this,' said Jim. 'I'm never much good at keeping my mouth shut. I'm so sorry.'

'Tell me.'

'Well, on the way up to Victoria on the train, we were kidding August about his girlfriend. We knew his mother was driving him round the bend, but he wouldn't make up his mind to propose to that Jean Tilverton.

'Then Nick said maybe he'd fancy a dancer in the show that evening. And when we were in the theatre and you came on in that wonderful fan dance, Nick said, 'How about that blonde, August?' And dared him to write you a note and ask you out.'

So even then — even *before* we'd met — that sod had been organizing my life.

I had not been August's choice.

I had been chosen for him by that bloody cowman.

Jim tutted again as he looked at my face.

'He did the right thing, Honey. August needed a prod and you are the perfect wife for him. We are all envious of him because of the girl he married. You must believe that.'

'Start the car,' I said. 'I don't want to hear any more.'

He started the engine and we went chugging off again towards the village.

'If it will make you feel any better,' said Jim, after a long silence, 'Brutus didn't like Nick, either.'

'Brutus?' I stared at his profile. 'Who on earth was Brutus?'

'A rather splendid bull which Mr Blake had in the old days and August inherited. The dairyman before Nick was good with Brutus. Used to take him out every day in good weather and tether him beside the track so he could see a bit of the world and graze to his heart's content until his services were needed.'

I could hear by the tone of his voice that something unpleasant was coming. But I wasn't surprised. If it concerned golden-boy Nick, it would be nasty — that was certain.

'Go on,' I said.

'During the winter months Brutus had that pen in the barn, where the calves are now, and soon after Nick took over Brutus cornered him in the pen and gored him.'

'What was Nick doing in the pen, for heaven's sake?'

Jim turned the car into his little car park.

'Nobody knows what he was doing inside the pen but August heard him screaming and raced to stick the hay fork into Brutus's flank, allowing Nick to roll out. He was quite badly injured and had to be taken to hospital. He was away for several weeks but couldn't remember what he was doing in there. Thought he'd gone to look at his ear, or something.'

'He could have done that from outside the pen,' I said. 'What happened to Brutus?'

'Taken away,' said Jim briefly, before

opening the door and climbing out. 'Here we are, Honey. Let's get your animals settled then I'll do my bit tomorrow.'

I bet he was taunting him, I thought, as we carried the cages through the office and on to the room beyond. I bet he was tormenting the creature and it turned on him. What a pity Brutus didn't do a better job. But I will repay.

Now there are three beings — me, Catty, and Brutus (five more if you count the kittens) who need to be avenged.

* * *

After Jim dropped me off and I'd walked with the empty cage up to the potting shed, I told Old Stow what I planned. He just grunted. He didn't show pleasure at seeing me around again. He didn't smile or look animated. But then, he seldom does.

I told him I'd be back to do the hens tomorrow and would come and see him afterwards. He grunted again. We had passed Mrs Stow on her bike just as we were leaving the village, and I had waved in a friendly fashion. I will have to explain my odd behaviour to the non-cat-lover tomorrow. I need her help with the cooking.

But first I have to sort out my husband.

As soon as I came in I went into the pink

bedroom and began to rearrange the bed linen. Vengeance is all very well — as saith the Lord — but it isn't fair to vent my wrath on August. He didn't inflict suffering on others. He might have sided with his bloody cowman but he hadn't actually *done* anything to my kittens, so I couldn't blame him too harshly.

Besides, I needed him on my side.

I am a woman, not unintelligent, although Mil might think otherwise, and I have plenty of time to plot and plan. There is no hurry. But WAR has been declared and August is going to help me, although he won't be aware of it.

I am going to punish that such-a-good-man-with-the-cows blond beast — just don't know how yet.

I need time to get an idea growing in my mind.

Tuesday evening

We are back together as husband and wife and I have apologized (sort of) to August for my actions. I think he understood in a vague way — he really only wants me to be happy and not to cause any more eruptions in the life on his farm.

I am learning to cook. I mean properly.

Mrs Stow is teaching me how to bake! Must write and tell Henry and Lyn.

Next time they visit I intend giving them a chocolate cake made by ME.

It has to be chocolate because that is August's favourite and I am going to seduce him all over again — with my *cooking*, not my dancing. There is still that wretched bill coming from Dylon and Sons so I have to get August nicely smoothed and satiated with his wife's amazing prowess, before I dare confess to my extravagances.

After that is done it will be time for Dairyman Nick and his come-uppance.

I don't suppose I can poison him, can I? No, too dangerous. Somebody else might eat what I had baked — anyway, I don't want him to die — just *suffer*.

Could I cry rape? People always believe the woman, don't they? But that would mean getting up close to that awful man — touching him — feeling his body against mine. No! Couldn't *ever* do that.

But there must be something — think, Honey, think . . .

25

Two or three weeks later? Not sure — anyway it's a Tuesday afternoon, I do know *that*.

All I've really done these past days is bake! I've had a go at Mrs Stow's scones and they haven't turned out too badly, although they were a bit hard. But it's the cake I have to get right for August.

I've done the hens every day and seen Old Stow to help with the weeding but he remains silent. I think he's still missing Catty. The other cats are still a bit distant with me. They haven't yet forgiven me for that traumatic journey down to the village and their operations.

Never mind, they are all safely home now — we won't have any more trouble from that COWMAN. He has yet to receive punishment. But my husband's stomach must come first.

Now I have made this gorgeous cake — even if I say so myself — but golly, did I have to practise to get it right!

Eggs and butter were fine but I had to borrow sugar from Betty and then from Mil, because I made so many mistakes. But the

FINAL ONE (and just in time for August's birthday tomorrow) is tremendous.

I know because it has risen just right, and when I tasted the wooden spoon it *tasted* just right.

Mrs Stow gave me enough lessons and when she stood beside me and watched and explained, I did perfectly. But I wanted to cook one entirely on my own to prove to August that I really am a splendid cook (and wife!) for him.

Attempt No. 1 without Mrs Stow, didn't rise. It looked more like a large biscuit, although it tasted jolly good.

I had to have Betty and Jerry to tea and we ate a lot of it. Then I sent the rest of it home with them wrapped in greaseproof paper. August must NOT KNOW.

Too hot an oven, said Mrs Stow, when I told her next day.

Wait, collect ingredients, start again.

Attempt No.2: Soggy in the middle and not very palatable. Not in for long enough, said Mrs Stow.

Most of that one went to Sarah and her neighbours. What wonderful creatures pigs are — not a crumb remained in two minutes flat. I had to make sure August was away and Dairyman Nick was occupied in the Milking Parlour before I went out to the sties. I wasn't going to have HIM seeing my mistake.

Attempt No.3 was made this morning and is absolutely fabulous. I've stuck the skewer down the middle like Mrs Stow told me, and it's come out as clean as a whistle. I've also licked the wooden spoon and it tasted scrumptious.

I asked Mrs Stow to go up and do the bedrooms and bathroom really well (for a change, although of course I didn't say that) and it gave me the opportunity to work away in the kitchen without being spied on.

Now all I have to do is hide it before tomorrow. It's August's birthday and he's promised to be in by four o'clock for his special tea party. I haven't told him more — it's going to be a surprise.

Mil is coming for supper, which Mrs Stow is helping me to prepare. All cold, thank goodness, so it will be easy to set out on that great oak table before she arrives. But the tea party is just for August and me and the splendid chocolate cake!

I'm going to lay the table in the kitchen — that's where August likes it best, although we'll have our evening meal in the dining room to please Mil. I'll look out the best china and wash it, and polish all the silver, and I've found some beautiful linen napkins.

But those are all for the evening.

For August and me we'll just have ordinary cups and plates and saucers and I've got five candles for the cake. It's not the full number but five will do as he's twenty-five tomorrow.

I'm also going to make proper hard-boiled egg and mayonnaise sandwiches (also his favourites) which I'll cut into neat little squares, and the cake will stand in the middle of the table.

As soon as I hear him taking off his boots I'll light the candles and start singing 'Happy Birthday'.

It will be the first we have celebrated together (mine isn't till November) — just the two of us. And hopefully next year, we will be three with a very small July adding to our family!

Tomorrow is going to be SPECIAL and maybe, once Mil has left us, and we have eaten and drunk to our entire satisfaction — and before I begin to seduce him! — I'll find the courage to tell him about that bill coming from Dylon and Sons.

Thursday

I really don't know how to go on — don't know what to say or how to say it. But I brought this book with me and I've always treated it as a friend — talked to it — written down things I wouldn't tell a living soul, so I suppose I'll have to go on and finish this tale. The sad story of Honey Brown's disastrous marriage to August Blake Esq.

Of course it had to be Nick, didn't it. From the very beginning when he 'chose' me, he was always the thorn in my flesh, the fly in my ointment, my bête noir.

What clichés those are, but I can't think of anything fresh or clever to say, I am exhausted both mentally and physically and don't know what to do with the rest of my life.

I am totally lost without August but must somehow live without him — exist, I suppose . . .

I am staying with Henry.

Dear kind Henry, who gave Lyn succour and strength in *her* hour of need and is doing the same for me now.

I couldn't go to Auntie.

She doesn't even know yet, though I will have to tell her soon before she contacts the farm and finds me gone.

I believe there is another girl living in that little slice of a room in Stanhope Gardens, anyway, and I don't know how to tell Auntie. Don't know how to explain — don't want loads of questions and having to find sensible answers.

Henry is easy.

I just phoned his office *praying* that he would be there — I knew he often worked late and then went out for the evening before returning to his flat — and he was still there.

I said, 'I need sanctuary. Can I come to you?'

And he said, 'Come.'

Funnily enough it was August who drove me to the station. I mean funny peculiar not funny ha ha.

We didn't speak. What was there to say in that cramped rattling space when both our minds were teeming with thoughts?

I had fully intended getting a taxi. Just flung a few essentials into a case, picked up this book which is, and will always remain *private*, looked into his top drawer and found some pound notes under his pile of handkerchiefs.

I don't care if it was stealing. I had discovered them when I put the ironing away. I hadn't been very annoyed, but I do remember thinking he has *some* cash so he could have given me more than a bob or two, if I'd asked.

But I never did ask and it doesn't matter now. I just took enough to pay for my fares and for living until I sorted myself out. Don't want to be beholden to Henry for *too* much.

After I'd gathered together everything that seemed necessary, I went down to the telephone in the hall and started to look for the taxi number. Then August strode in.

'Where are you going?' he said, looking at the coat over my arm and my bag and suitcase.

'London,' I said.

'I'll take you.'

So I put down the phone and carried my stuff outside. I wasn't going to look for the truck. I wasn't going to risk seeing that COWMAN again. So I waited for August to bring the car round, as they say in novels.

Henry is such a good friend. He asked on the phone about what time to expect me; I had fully intended to sit and wait on his doorstep as he is such a busy man. But as soon as the taxi dropped me off, his front door opened and he ushered me inside. He took my case and led the way up the stairs to his flat.

'Do you want to talk?' was all he asked.

'No,' I said. 'I want to sleep and sleep and then to think. I need time and space, Henry. But I'll tell you once I've recovered. Promise.'

He nodded. 'There'll be a bite to eat in half an hour. Come and join me, Honey. Then you can have a bath and fall into bed.'

Fortunately he is away all day, which is

another reason I phoned him and not Auntie. He didn't come to my room this morning with a 'nice cup of tea' at some ungodly hour. He must have left the house soon after nine, so now I have all the time and peace I need in which to think.

He told me last night that Freda doesn't come in on Thursdays so I slept late. Freda is a refugee from Poland and comes in twice a week to 'do' for him. She speaks very little English and I've only met her once when she and her sister acted as waitresses at one of Henry's parties.

This flat is so different to the farm! It is warm and fully carpeted and very well equipped in every way. No draughts, no bare floor-boards, no smelly dogs. It is on the first floor of a big house in Lower Sloane Street, just a few minutes from Sloane Square Underground.

It is elegantly furnished and there are two spare bedrooms — one which I now inhabit — but Henry has never had a companion either male or female, since I have known him. He has loads of acquaintances but few close friends. That is why it was especially nice of him to make the effort to come down to Sussex to see me, and that he supports both Lyn and me when we're in trouble.

* * *

I'm trying to think what I should do next but I keep remembering the cats, and the hens, and Old Stow. What is happening to them now I've gone?

I try not to think about August. I'd rather not. But what has he told Mil? And Betty? And Mrs Stow? They must be asking about me.

Did he eat my chocolate cake? Or did he leave it sitting in the middle of the kitchen table with its five candles?

Did Mrs Stow see it there? What did she think? And Mil was coming for his birthday supper. Did he put her off?

Heavens what drama!

Ex-showgirl Honey Brown has caused tumult in many people's lives. How is her husband going to explain her sudden departure? It was bad enough when she created chaos over those kittens. What *is* she up to now?

August will have to lie, won't he. But what will he say?

I'd better go and get myself a bit of toast and a coffee. And have another ciggy. At least I can buy those easily here. Then tomorrow I'll talk to Henry. I'll feel stronger then and he has a right to know. I'll tell him everything — he is worldly and so wise — ask him what I should do with the rest of my life.

26

Friday

Henry isn't free this evening so I took the opportunity to phone Auntie.

All I said was that I was in town for a short break and was seeing a few old friends. I asked which days would suit her next week because that will give me time to consider what to tell her. She said Thursday.

'Do you want to tell me what this is really about, Annie?' she went on. 'I know you very well, dear child, and you don't sound happy to me.'

I hesitated, not knowing how to reply, not wanting to pour out the sordid details over the phone. I needed to see her, face to face, to choose my words carefully and consider how much I was prepared to say.

'I'll tell you when I see you,' I said. 'I'm staying with Henry at present so you could come here to Lower Sloane Street, if you like. Or shall I come to you?'

'You come to me,' she said. 'Eleven o'clock sharp.'

I could hear from her voice that she was

dying to know more and questions were queuing up on her tongue, so I put the phone down quickly after agreeing.

Not Auntie yet.

First I have to have Henry's reaction.

Saturday afternoon

This morning Henry took the day off. Well, the morning, anyway. He said he couldn't go through another day wondering what had happened to me, and we'd both be fresher in the morning.

So, with a mug of good strong Nescafé in my hand, and a hot chocolate for Henry (he says he became addicted to hot chocolate after reading so many Hercule Poirot novels) we sat in his elegant sitting room; me on the sofa, he on the chair opposite, with the low glass-topped table between us.

'I always disliked that Dairyman Nick,' I said, 'and even more when he drowned my kittens. I was determined to punish him but had to have August on my side.

'So I learned how to make cakes from Mrs Stow and baked this gorgeous chocolate cake for his birthday. I wanted to prove what an accomplished cook I was, and also wanted to give him a lovely birthday surprise on

Wednesday and get him in a good mood.

'I'd laid the table and put the cake in the middle and was waiting for him to come in for tea.'

'And?' said Henry, sipping at his mug of chocolate, as I paused.

'He didn't come,' I said, trying to warm my fingers around the coffee in my hand. 'He *promised* he'd be in by four so I waited and waited. But by half past I thought he must have forgotten and I went to look for him.'

Waves of anger, of horror, of misery, washed over me.

'Go on,' said Henry.

Taking a deep breath I tried to control my thudding heart.

'I found him in the back of the barn with Nick. His trousers were down and they were — he was . . . Nick saw me over August's shoulder and he *laughed*, Henry! He was fondling my husband and he shouted out, 'There's Mrs Honey! Coming to join us, are you?'

'I turned and ran. I was so shocked and revolted all I could do was run indoors and up the stairs and grab a suitcase. I wanted OUT, Henry!'

Slamming my mug down on the glass-topped table I spilt some of the contents.

'I didn't *know* August. After six months of

loving him I didn't *know* he was that way. I still can't believe what I saw — I just don't understand. He was my *husband*, Henry.'

I was fumbling for a cigarette but — 'Have a brandy,' said Henry, getting up and walking over to the drinks trolley, where he poured out a generous amount. 'Drink this.' He removed the cigarettes and placed the glass firmly in my hand. Then he leaned over and wiped up my spilt coffee with his handkerchief.

I couldn't cry any more. I had cried ever since I had been at Henry's but now all the moisture has been drained out of me. The brandy (normally I hate brandy) was surprisingly comforting and for the moment I didn't need a ciggy.

'Do you still love him?'

'I don't know,' I said.

I feel numb, hopeless, disbelieving, yes, and still angry. How could I have been so stupid? How could I not have known? But love him? I don't know about that.

'I wonder what he told his mother,' said Henry. 'I wonder what folk in the village are saying. Mrs Stow must have spread the news of your departure — but what is the reason they give, I wonder.'

I frowned. 'You don't appear surprised, Henry. Did you guess?'

'I scarcely know August,' he said. 'How can I judge?'

I didn't dare ask if he were queer. There is something still about Henry. Something contained and controlled deep inside him. He doesn't show his emotions so one really is never sure what is going on in his mind.

'You've been in the theatre world for so long — you must have known several homosexuals, even if they kept their actions secret. How could August marry me, Henry, *knowing* what he was?'

'He probably wants children,' said Henry. 'Family to inherit the farm.'

'But what about *me*?' I said, as anger began to burn again. 'What about me and how *I* felt? What about his *wife*?'

'No doubt he hoped you wouldn't find out. I'm sure he loves you, Honey, in his way. Poor Oscar loved his wife and sons, you know.'

'And look what happened to *him*!' I shouted. 'I don't want to find myself married to a criminal!'

'That's better,' said Henry. 'Anger gives you strength.'

I ignored that comment. 'My cats will be missing me, and Old Stow, and Betty. What will they all be thinking?'

'You must speak to August,' said Henry. 'Phone him and ask him to come here. Then you will be able to talk quietly and in private and discuss things properly away from the farm. You need to find out the reason he has given for your flight, and whether he wants you back. Then you will know where you stand and *you* can make the final decision.'

'I'll think about it,' I said.

* * *

I know Henry was trying to console me but I remain upset. I don't want to telephone August. I don't want to talk to him. Not yet. I don't know *what* I want to do — I just keep remembering and remembering.

Did he ever really love me? Were all those kisses and caresses and tender words just an act?

Or did he imagine Nick in his arms when he held me?

But our bodies are different — the very act of love is different. How can he have pretended I was his cowman?

Oh God, why did he marry me? Why did he ruin both our lives when all he wanted was that cowman's embraces?

I suppose he tried to appear normal. For his mother's sake. For the farm's sake. He couldn't dare let the village know that he was queer.

And children? How *could* he be a good father and teach them proper morals when he was lusting after that blond peasant?

He'll be ostracized from society if the truth comes out — laughed at in the pub and at the market. He couldn't bear the sneering and humility and disgrace of being 'one of those'. *And* he could be sent to prison.

If she knew, Mil might forgive him. He is her only child and she does love him. But the shock and shame of his behaviour becoming public knowledge would affect her badly.

So I was a necessary distraction. Honey Brown was the perfect little wife to cover his sins.

I'm starting to cry again and smudging these pages, but I *loved* him — and I really thought he loved me.

As the tears flow again I feel totally bewildered. Why is this happening to me? Why did I fall in love with him?

Because of Dairyman Nick, of course, if the truth be known. He decided — he chose me.

So August Blake married me to please his bloody cowman.

I must stop now and try to sleep — allow these soggy pages to dry out.

Damn, damn, and blast you, August Blake, and your wretched unnatural desires . . .

27

Wednesday

Mil has made the first move. A letter arrived for me this morning; I know her handwriting.

August hasn't told her the truth. How could he? He can't admit to an act which is against the law.

I'm sure now that I was chosen as the safe option. Jean Tilverton, a well educated and well respected teacher, might have guessed at her husband's homosexual affair with his cowman.

But little Honey Brown would be much easier to fool. So Dairyman Nick 'chose' me. And even if I *had* discovered the truth about August's illicit activities why should it have bothered me? I must have been used to all those queers hanging around in the theatre, mustn't I?

Well, Mr Bloody Dairyman Nick, you thought *wrong*. And silly little Honey Brown is not going to be so easily fooled, or appeased.

* * *

When I opened Mil's letter, wondering what on earth I was going to read all she said was:

'Please see August and sort out your difficulties, dear. I know marriage is not easy, and your life down here was very different to the one you were used to in town. But you were so *good* for August, and he misses you so much, and so do I. Please come back, dear, and talk things over before making any fatal decisions . . . '

'He's missing you so much!' I said to Henry, when he came in. 'Pah! I'm not going back to August if that sodomite is there. Do you know, I wanted to poison him, only I was scared August or Mrs Stow might eat what I had made. And that was *before* I knew about his sexual link with my husband.'

'You are sounding like the old Honey now,' said Henry. 'Pity you didn't get rid of him. But we couldn't have you hanged for his murder, could we.' He paused, assessing my expression as he waited for an answer. 'Could you still make a life with August knowing what you do now?'

Henry had asked me this before and I had been unable to answer him. Was I any clearer in my mind today?

Then I thought about our week in Wales, and of the times I seduced him with my high heels and stockings and suspenders. I remembered his long strong body and Gregory Peck smile. I did still love him although I wished I didn't. But did he still love me? Or could he still *pretend* to love me? I wasn't sure that I could bear it now.

'I might go back if he asked me,' I said. 'But not with that man there. *Never* with that cowman about.'

Henry nodded. 'In which case, stay here, Honey. There is no hurry. Wait and see what transpires. I am always glad to have your company.'

'What shall I say to Mil?' Dear Henry, I am really clinging to him now, for mental support, physical comfort, and wise, impartial advice.

'Tell her you need time in which to consider,' he said. 'And go to class again. Forget your emotions for a while and get your body moving. Don't forget I can get you work, if you want it.'

Thursday

Henry has made me plan for the next day even if I can't plan for the years ahead. I still have plenty of August's money so I took the Underground to Tottenham Court Road this morning and made my way to Dean Street. I bought a new leotard and tights and flat ballet shoes — but no point shoes. It's been many months since I've taken part in a ballet class and I don't fancy point work just yet.

At the Windmill there was a big practice room upstairs, which I told Betty about. It has huge wall mirrors so we could watch every movement of our bodies, and we used to limber up there before the first show of the day, or learn new routines before rehearsing on stage.

But for a proper class we all had our favourite teacher. Mine was Freddie Stropp.

Freddie teaches from a studio on the first floor of a building full of music and dancing, just off Leicester Square, and he gives classes every morning (except Saturdays and Sundays) from ten to twelve.

I always enjoyed Freddie's vigorous method of teaching in the old days, and intend going to class tomorrow. Freddie is a small, squat man, with a loud voice who cannot dance himself. But he knows exactly what he wants and manages to obtain excellent results from his eager, sweating students.

Friday

I went to Freddie's this morning and really wished I hadn't. The mirrors showed my disgusting stomach and Freddie wasn't kind to me.

'Where have you been, Honey?' he said, at the end of class. 'Haven't seen you for months and I'm afraid it shows, darling. Didn't you get wed, or something? I heard you'd left the Mill. If you want to work again you'll have to get rid of that fat and come to class for several weeks before anyone will look at you, darling.'

'Henry says he can find me work,' I said, knowing Freddie spoke the truth but annoyed by his dismissive attitude.

'Has Henry seen you like this? Has he seen you dance?'

'Not yet. But I'm going to work hard and get back into shape,' I said.

Freddie shrugged and raised his eyebrows, before turning to speak to a lovely lithe young dancer who I hadn't seen before.

But then I had been away for too long. I had lost my figure and my strength in this dancing world, and my baby and my husband in the other. Where did I really want to live? Where did I truly belong?

All the way back to Henry's flat I pondered.

Did I want to dance again? To strive for success? To perform the daily rigours of a class and be shouted at by Freddie? Did I want to compete again and fight every inch of the way for a slender body and fast-moving legs?

Or did I want a life in the countryside with animals, and gardening, and cooking, and a husband who loved another man more than me?

* * *

When I arrived back in Lower Sloane Street, August was waiting on the doorstep. He stunned me once again with his Gregory Peck hair and lop-sided smile, his long corduroy and tweed-jacketed body and his pleading eyes.

'Please let me come in, Honey,' he said. 'I must talk to you.'

There was only a small table in Henry's kitchen, with one chair. I don't think he did much cooking, although he gave me excellent meals, mainly from Harrods' Food Hall. So we took our drinks — coffee for me, tea for August — through to the elegant sitting room.

I could feel my heart banging away like a steam engine beneath my cotton top, but I willed myself to keep calm.

'I told everyone you had left because of the kittens,' August said, sitting down in the armchair opposite me on the sofa. 'I said you'd had a row with Nick, and that you were upset about the cats and stormed out.' He looked down at his tea cup. 'It was all I could think of and everyone believed me.'

Old Stow knew how upset I was about Catty, and Mil and Betty and Jim all knew. But that had happened weeks ago.

'Why should I suddenly leave when all that was over and done with weeks ago?'

'I said you held it against Nick. And when you saw him in the yard one day you had a go at him and he retaliated. I had to think of *something*,' he said, his voice rising. 'All those people were asking — even Jim Folder. I had to give them a reason, Honey.'

'So it was all my fault? Silly little Honey runs away because of a minor tiff with the cowman? Why couldn't *you* have taken the blame? Why couldn't you have told them you'd beaten me, or got drunk and assaulted me, or something violent like that? But they wouldn't have believed you, would they? And as you couldn't give them the real reason for my departure, you made up lies and made me take the blame.'

I grabbed my pack of cigarettes and tried

to stuff one in my mouth, but it was hard to hold with my bottom lip quivering.

August's eyebrows drew together. 'Please come back,' he said. 'Mother has moved in again and she's driving me crazy.'

'Tough titty, August,' I said, removing my unlit cigarette. 'If you had the courage to tell *her* the truth, you'd soon get rid of her.'

'You know I can't do that.'

'What about your boyfriend? Is he staying?'

'Yes. I can't give him up.' August's eyes were as black as his brows.

Then anger came to strengthen me again — so much better than tears.

'How *dare* you say that to me! And how dare you marry me! You knew all along what you were, August Blake, yet you pretended to love me, and promised to love me forever in church, and in front of all those people! And you knew it was a farce. How could you?'

I tried to light my cigarette again but my hand was shaking.

'Here, let me.' August leaned across the table and lit my ciggy before sitting back down again. 'I didn't pretend, Honey. I do love you but in a different way. Please come back and you won't see anything unpleasant, I promise. Just come home and we'll make a new life together. We'll have children.'

Henry had been right. August did want a

family. So did I, oh, so did I.

'I can't come back,' I said, managing to inhale a little. 'I'll never return if that man is there.'

August stood up and came round to sit next to me. He reached for my hand but I pulled it away.

'Nick won't go,' he said softly, 'and I don't want him to. But I love you both, Honey. Please come and we'll work something out.'

I rose on rather shaky feet and carried my mug through to the kitchen. August followed me.

'You can't have it both ways,' I said. 'It's either a wife and children, or your cowman friend. You decide, August Blake.'

Then I opened the front door and told him to go.

* * *

When Henry came in I had to tell him what had happened because he could see I'd been crying. Again. Stupid woman. I just couldn't stop.

'More brandy,' said Henry, giving me another glass of that comforting stuff. Then he said a surprising thing. 'You know, Honey, that young man could cause a lot of trouble if he was forced to leave the farm.'

'What do you mean?'

'I mean that August can't give him the sack, even if he wanted to. He is good at his job, isn't he? If August handed him his notice what excuse could he give? There is no reason for dismissal. And if he doesn't wish to go, he could cause August any amount of trouble by talking his mouth off.'

'But Nick wouldn't want anyone knowing the truth!' I stared at Henry. 'What they are doing is against the law!'

'Why should Nick care? He could say August seduced him. He could say August employed him with just such a purpose in mind. He could play the innocent and August would be arrested for breaking the Sexual Offences Act.

'That Nick is a dangerous young man, Honey, and you may have to accept his presence if he doesn't wish to go, and *you* want to return to August.'

* * *

No, no, no, I *cannot* accept that. I will never return if that lout is there.

I cannot sleep and keep thinking of what Henry said, and what August said, and I have to keep writing down my thoughts.

I want children so much — and I do love

August even knowing what I do.

But I CANNOT accept that cowman — not on the farm — not within my sight. I cannot bear him.

So how can this problem ever be solved?

I must go and get some more brandy — then perhaps I can sleep.

28

Thursday evening

I went to see Auntie this morning at eleven o'clock.

I was dreading the visit, but once I was with her again and sitting in her familiar over-crowded, bed/sitting room with a lovely strong mug of Nescafé, I began to relax.

I didn't smoke because she had never allowed it in her home but I was dying for a ciggy.

'Who is in that room?' I said, jerking my head towards the tiny little room across the hallway, which I had occupied after leaving the Home and before finding work at the Windmill and my new digs in Barkston Gardens.

'Rosemary,' said Auntie. 'She is nice and very quiet and works as a secretary in some big firm in Liverpool Street. She's away all day and as there is a canteen at her work she only needs a light meal here in the evenings. So we don't clash in the kitchen.'

I nodded and sipped at my coffee, remembering the trouble I had had trying to keep out of Auntie's way when I was a full-time student at Miss Griggs'. I used to take sandwiches and a flask in my holdall, but after a day's vigorous exercise I was always starving on my return to Stanhope Gardens.

If Auntie was out (which she usually was) I used to scurry into the kitchen and make myself a huge fry-up with two eggs, two slices of fried bread and a tomato if there was one. Auntie always had eggs and a bowl of lard in the meat-safe, left over from the Sunday joint. But bacon was a rarity in those days.

I would open the window and flap the drying up cloth up and down to try and get rid of the smells. Auntie wasn't keen on fry-ups, herself.

When I'd finished the meal in my room, I'd race back to the kitchen, wash up all the greasy utensils, dry them, put them away, put the kettle on and make a coffee, then I'd close the window, and get back to my room before she returned.

That was why my own room at Mrs Walker's had been such a welcome change. I could smoke whenever I wanted, without having to open a window afterwards and flap.

'Now tell me,' said Auntie, sitting opposite and looking across her big round (also cluttered) table with her light, penetrating eyes. 'Tell me what's wrong, Annie.'

I told her the truth. I had never lied to her and felt she would understand my flight better if I explained exactly what I had seen. Although it still made me feel sick just to think about it.

Auntie didn't appear shocked. But then she seldom portrayed emotion — a bit like Henry.

'Pity,' was all she said. 'He's a good man, Annie.'

'It's not only August,' I said hotly, 'it's that awful cowman, Nick. I cannot bear him.'

Then I told her about August's visit up to town and what he had said.

'So he still loves you in his own way,' she said. 'Are you going back, Annie?'

'I don't know. Henry says he can find me work if I want to dance again.'

Auntie poured herself another cup of tea.

'Think long and hard,' she said. 'Your August can offer you a secure and comfortable home, which is more than the theatre can promise. Oh, I know you are young,' she said, lifting her hand as I attempted to interrupt her, 'and have several years of performing ahead of you. But what then, Annie? What will you do when other girls come forward to take your parts, and auditions become less and less successful? Will you have the money to open a studio?

Will you be able to teach?'

I thought of Betty Folder and her idea of giving dancing classes in the village. I could do *that* as I grew older and if I returned to August. But there was always Dairyman Nick blocking my way and, if Henry had been right, Nick was never going to leave. So, stale-mate.

I left Stanhope Gardens with my mind still in turmoil but promised Auntie I would let her know my final decision. What am I going to do?

Tuesday afternoon

I've been going to regular classes with Freddie Stropp for almost two weeks now but he remains sarcastic, which is doing nothing for my self-esteem, and I am growing more and more depressed.

What shall I do?

I need a sign. I need someone to say, Honey, this is what you must do.

It isn't fair to keep begging Henry for advice. This is *my* life. August is *my* husband. And I jolly well have to make up my own mind.

Except I can't.

Sometimes I remember Jim Folder saying,

'You are a strong girl, Honey, and you disappoint me,' after my kittens died. I wish *he* was here now. He would know what to do.

But there I go again, expecting someone else to make the final decision for me.

Come on, Honey, you learnt how to bake that wonderful cake — though what a disaster that achievement turned out to be! And you learnt how to look after the hens, and how to bottle fruit, and how to help Old Stow in the garden — and you cooked splendid Sunday roasts.

You learnt and mastered all those new things, but they were all on the farm. Does your future lie there?

But what about that bloody cowman? I didn't succeed in punishing him, or getting rid of him, did I?

Back to square one, and another ciggy, and a slurp of brandy.

Wednesday

Another bad night but this morning: EUREKA!

I cannot believe it. I've had another letter from Mil and she says Dairyman Nick has *gone*!

I haven't been to class — haven't done

anything except read and re-read her letter. I am so afraid I'm misunderstanding what she says — that I'm imagining it — that I'm reading what my eyes want me to see.

* * *

Now I've given it to Henry — he came home early, thank God — and he's reading it and I'm sitting here scribbling down my thoughts because I've got to do *something* until he tells me it's true . . .

* * *

Three hours later

It is true.

'She begs you to return,' said Henry. 'She says August is miserable and she cannot lift him from the Slough of Despond. She says first he lost his wife and now he's lost his dairyman, and he is totally bereft. She can do nothing with him and the farm is suffering. She is doing her best to manage but please, please, come back, Honey.'

Henry smiled and looked across at me over the pages in his hand.

'There you are. Does that answer your problem, Honey?'

'Why did Nick leave? She doesn't say that,

does she? Why do you think he's gone? You said he'd never leave. I'm not going back if he's likely to return at any moment.'

Excitement was beginning to grow in my chest as I reached for another ciggy. Was this the sign? Had God worked some amazing miracle and removed that peasant from my path? Was it possible?

'He won't come back,' said Henry.

I snorted. 'You can't know that. August told me he would never leave and even *you* said it wouldn't be easy to get rid of him in case he talked about his relationship with August. But he has kept his mouth shut because Mil would have known, otherwise.'

'Nick won't be returning to the farm,' said Henry, and there was something in his voice which alerted me, even though his face remained expressionless.

It wasn't God. It was Henry.

'What have you done?' I said, staring at him.

'Don't ask, Honey. I have contacts in many professions and I am fond of you. I won't have you upset if I can help it.'

I was speechless. Henry couldn't have *killed* him. He was too far away and there wasn't a body. Mil would have said if there were suspicious circumstances.

So what had happened to him? Henry had

had something to do with his disappearance — but what? I had to know.

'I must know what has happened to the man,' I said. 'I must know where he is and whether he'll come back one day. He might be hovering somewhere in the village and — '

'You need know nothing,' said Henry, quite sharply for him. 'The man has gone and that is all there is to it.' He lifted Mil's letter.

'She says she's interviewing now — August is not interested — and she thinks she has found a young chap with a nice little wife who seems very suitable. They both love the cottage and his references are good. So there — *that* is what you need to know, Honey. Now, are you going back?'

I looked at him for a long time and he looked back. Not an insolent stare — nothing cringe-making — simply determined. He had asked me a question and wanted an answer. The choice was mine. Take it, or leave it. Farm or stage. Make up your mind, Honey.

I took a deep breath. 'I'm going back,' I said.

'August won't change,' said Henry.

'I know that. But with that awful cowman out of the way I want to see if we can live together again. Like we did before — like he said we could. It'll be hard for both of us but I want to give it a try.'

Henry shrugged but said nothing more and I came in here and began packing.

I shall go on Friday. I'm not going to telephone or say anything to anyone — I'm just going to arrive and take it from there. I still have enough money left over for a taxi from Horsham station so that will be fine.

I'm really feeling quite excited; it is the right thing to do — I'm sure of it . . .

29

Sunday evening

Before leaving for his office on Friday, Henry phoned for a taxi then kissed my cheek briefly as we waited together on the pavement.

'Good luck, Honey,' he said.

Remembering now, I feel guilty that I didn't say something. That I didn't thank him properly for his kindness, and his friendship, during the past difficult weeks. But I was so intent on my plan, so relieved at having finally made up my mind to return to the farm, that poor Henry was put to one side.

All I could think about was getting back to August and settling into my old routine with no frightful Dairyman Nick disturbing my contentment. I wanted to pick up the threads again and prove to August that I could make him happy, and that we could build a new, stronger life together in Sussex.

But I will show Henry my gratitude one day. I'll ask him down to the farm when I know

August will be out, and we'll talk and remember together and it'll be like the old days.

But not yet. There is so much to sort out first.

⋆ ⋆ ⋆

I may not have time to sit and scribble in this diary from now on, but I shall keep it. It is, after all, a detailed account of the first six dramatic months in the life of Honey Blake née Brown.

Whether anyone else will ever read it I don't know. It is so very personal and must remain secret at present. So I'm going to take it up to the box room and place it at the bottom of a suitcase, well hidden from prying eyes or inquisitive fingers. The case will be locked but *I* will always know it is there and where to find the key . . .

The best moment — the one I will keep, like Mary, and ponder it in my heart — was when the taxi from Horsham dropped me off at the farm on Friday.

I had timed it for early afternoon, so Mrs Stow had gone home when I walked into the kitchen.

Mil was not there, thank goodness, but August was sitting slumped at the table with his head in his hands. The dogs were at his feet.

As I entered, Wolf pricked her ears and gazed at me with her yellow eyes but August appeared not to have heard me and Reg remained sleeping.

'I've come back,' I said, and Wolf's tail began to move gently on the floor. 'I've come back,' I said more loudly, putting down my case. 'If you still want me?'

August lifted his head and stared. Then he swung round in his chair and held out his arms. I walked forward and stood very close as his arms went round my body and he buried his face in my stomach.

Putting my hands on either side of his head, I bent and pressed my lips against his thick dark hair.

Beautiful man, weak man, flawed being. Yet he was my husband and I loved him. On the train journey down to Horsham I had decided that I could accept his homosexual needs just so long as I never saw, or knew, any of his male friends. And so long as he really tried to make me happy. He had said he loved me on that visit to Henry's flat, so he would have to continually prove it to me.

When Mil returned, she found us both sitting at the table with wet faces, drinking cups of tea.

Wednesday evening (haven't quite finished!)

I don't know what has happened to Dairyman Nick. I can't talk about him to August. In fact, by unspoken agreement, we haven't discussed his sexuality at all. And I trust him to keep any further male attachments well away from the farm.

Mil told me she had alerted the police to Nick's disappearance and they had come and had a nose round. It was all very odd, they said, and he was now registered as a missing person.

'He didn't leave a note,' she said, shaking her head, 'and hasn't been in contact since that Thursday night. But he took a suitcase and all his belongings with him. The only thing he left behind were his ferrets. Poor things, luckily I noticed them still in their cage so I've been feeding them. And the new young man, Bob, says he'll look after them until Nick comes to collect them.'

I don't care about the ex-cowman and hope he never returns for his ferrets. But I still think about Catty and hope one day she will come back to us.

The other cats gave me a great welcome, as did Old Stow on Monday. Well, not hugely enthusiastic — not like Mrs Stow's joy on seeing me again. But he grunted through his gums and said he was glad the hoeing would be done again. The weeds were growing something terrible.

Betty and Jerry came up yesterday and Betty says Jim is *so* relieved that I've come back to August. Wonder if he knew deep down that something was going on between those two? Won't think about it; it's over now — thank God. At least with *that* man.

Tomorrow I'm going down to see Mrs Dawson and will find out about hiring the church hall for dancing classes. Mil says she will play the piano for me (yet another of her many talents) and when we can find the time, she's going to teach me to drive her car!

My life has taken a decisive turn for the better and I know it was right to come back here.

As Henry told me, August will never change, but he is determined to try and make me happy and *I* am going to try even harder to make him a good wife.

He'll have to get used to leading two separate lives but he must have been used to that in the past with Mil, so he should be able to carry on now with his new family, so long as he takes care.

Mil has returned to her bungalow and August and I are more relaxed in each other's company — it is so *good* to be home!

I love him and know that he loves me in his own way. I managed to conceive before — even though I lost the baby — here's hoping and praying that we will be able to have little July next year . . .

Other titles published by
The House of Ulverscroft:

SCHRODER

Amity Gaige

As an adolescent, Erik Schroder — a first-generation East German immigrant — adopts a new name and a new persona in the hope that it will help him fit in. This fateful white lie will set him on an improbably and ultimately tragic course. Years later, amid a heated custody battle with his estranged wife, Erik kidnaps his six-year-old daughter, Meadow . . . From the confines of a correctional facility, Erik relates the story of their seven days on the road as he tries to outrun the authorities, and surveys the course of his life in an attempt to understand and explain his behaviour . . .

AN INVISIBLE SIGN OF MY OWN

Aimee Bender

When Mona Grey is ten, her father contracts a mysterious illness. His gradual withdrawal marks a similar change in Mona, who removes herself from anything — or anyone — that might bring her happiness. Numbers provide a kind of solace, and help her make sense of the world. As a maths teacher, Mona delights her pupils by encouraging them to find objects that take the form of numbers. But when seven-year-old Lisa appears with a zero that speaks of real turmoil, Mona realises she must find a way to reconnect with the world she has been afraid of for so long . . .

BAR BALTO

Faiza Guene and Sarah Ardizzone

Joel, AKA 'the Rink' because he's so bald you could skate on it, is the very unpopular owner of the only bar in town — so unpopular that when he is found dead, it's not so much a question of who did kill him as who didn't. His customers certainly had plenty of motives . . . In a series of monologues, the locals tell us their stories in their own, very different voices. As the tension mounts and we're still none the wiser, the ending — in the form of Joel's final confession — is as shocking and tragic as it is unexpected.

SIGNS OF LIFE

Anna Raverat

Ten years ago, Rachel had an affair. It spiralled out of control and left her and her life in pieces. Now, writing at her window, she tries to put those pieces back together. She has her memories, recollections of dreams and her old yellow notebook. More than anything she wants to be honest. She knows that her memory is patchy and her notebook incomplete. But there is something else. Something terrible happened to her lover. Her account is hypnotic, delicate, disquieting and bold. But is she telling the truth?

THE TASTE OF APPLE SEEDS

Katharina Hagena with Jamie Bulloch

For Iris, childhood memories are of long, hot summers spent playing with her cousin Rosmarie in their grandmother's garden. When her grandmother dies, Iris inherits the property — along with her family's darkest secrets. Reluctant to keep it, but reluctant to sell, Iris spends one last summer at the house. In the flicker between remembrance and forgetting, she recalls an enigmatic grandfather who came back from war a different man; the night her cousin Rosmarie fell through the conservatory roof and shattered her family's lives; and a moment of love that made all the trees in the orchard bloom overnight . . .

BORN WEIRD

Andrew Kaufman

The Weirds have always been peculiar. Annie, their grandmother, had given each of her five grandchildren a special power that she thought was a blessing. Richard, the oldest, always keeps safe; Abba always has hope; Lucy is never lost and Kent can beat anyone in a fight. As for Angie, she always forgives, instantly. But these blessings have proved to be curses and ruined their lives. Now Annie is dying she has one last task for Angie. She must bring her siblings to her Grandmother's hospital room, so that when she dies she can lift these blessings turned curses.